S0-DOR-450

SEP - - 2023

REBECCA REZNIK REBOOTS the UNIVERSE

ReBecca RezniK ReBoots the UniVeRSe

Samara ShanKer

Atheneum Books for Young Readers
NEW YORK LONDON TORONTO SYDNEY NEW DELHI

atheneum

ATHENEUM BOOKS FOR YOUNG READERS

An imprint of Simon & Schuster Children's Publishing Division

1230 Avenue of the Americas, New York, New York 10020

This book is a work of fiction. Any references to historical events, real people, or real places are used fictitiously. Other names, characters, places, and events are products of the author's imagination, and any resemblance to actual events or places or persons, living or dead, is entirely coincidental.

Text © 2023 by Samara Shanker

Jacket illustration © 2023 by Shane Cluskey

Jacket design by Greg Stadnyk © 2023 by Simon & Schuster, Inc.

All rights reserved, including the right of reproduction in whole or in part in any form.

ATHENEUM BOOKS FOR YOUNG READERS is a registered trademark of Simon & Schuster, Inc. Atheneum logo is a trademark of Simon & Schuster, Inc.

For information about special discounts for bulk purchases, please contact Simon & Schuster Special Sales at 1-866-506-1949 or business@simonandschuster.com.

The Simon & Schuster Speakers Bureau can bring authors to your live event. For more information or to book an event, contact the Simon & Schuster Speakers Bureau at 1-866-248-3049 or visit our website at www.simonspeakers.com.

Interior design by Irene Metaxatos

The text for this book was set in ITC Bookman Std.

Manufactured in the United States of America

0723 FFG

First Edition

10 9 8 7 6 5 4 3 2 1

CIP data for this book is available from the Library of Congress.

ISBN 9781665935234

ISBN 9781665935258 (ebook)

For Sahana.
Use that conviction for good.
And take your time.

—S. S.

REBECCA
REZNIK
REBOOTS
the
UNIVERSE

1

GROWING PAINS

As a rule, Rebecca Reznik did not like change. This made being thirteen somewhat difficult, and not just in the horrifyingly embarrassing "your body is changing" kind of way, like when Becca first got her period and her mother subjected her to a mortifyingly thorough explanation of her biological systems while Becca's brother, Jake, made loud vomiting noises outside the closed bedroom door. Not even in the way that high school and its overwhelming number of people and their overwhelming amounts of noise and smells and expectations were looming terrifyingly closer with each passing day. It was difficult like this:

They're fighting again.

The plain text in its blue bubble looked very serious in the space underneath the barrage of ridiculous GIFs her friend Eitan had last sent in the Best Friends group chat. Naomi, predictably, was the first to respond.

Parents always fight. It's NBD Becks.

Not mine, not like this.

I think they probably did, and we were just too little to notice, Eitan replied. **Or maybe they're less careful about hiding it from us because we're teenagers now.**

It's loud.

The complaint felt silly, but it was the truth, even if it didn't quite cover the way the raised voices and the harsher pitch to the words grated on Becca's ears in a near-painful way. It wasn't that she couldn't handle loud noises—she had three younger siblings; her house was never quiet—but the quality of this loudness was different. It hurt. Naomi's response came quickly once again.

Do you need to come over here?

Something warm settled in Becca's chest at how much her friends understood all the things she wasn't quite able to say. She desperately wanted to say yes. It was pizza night at the Teitelbaum house, and Naomi's mama always managed to get the cheese exactly the same texture of melty every time. It was great. But—

I don't think I can ask right now.

Just go and beg forgiveness later? Eitan suggested.

Not when they're in this mood.

Naomi responded with a string of eloquent emojis that expressed her frustration with the situation. Becca snorted.

I'll be fine. I'll see you guys tomorrow.

You're sure? Becca could almost see the dubious look on Eitan's face that she knew would be accompanying the message.

Yeah. Becca took a deep breath. She was thirteen now, almost fourteen. She'd had her Bat Mitzvah and everything, so she was basically a grown-up. She could do her homework while her parents yelled downstairs. **Like you said,** she sent, **it's probably just that the munchkins are out of the house for sports so they're not being quiet. It'll be fine. I'm sure they'll chill in a bit.**

It felt like hollow reassurance even as she sent it, but Eitan and Naomi seemed to accept it since the conversation turned to other things, like what everyone was hoping to get for Hanukkah and the gift Eitan was supposed to be allowed to open that night—several nights early because his parents had a surprise for him. Becca flipped her phone over, not feeling like meeting her friends' enthusiasm about the upcoming holiday, and turned the white noise machine in her room up to its loudest setting.

Eitan was waiting for Becca in front of the school the next day, standing on the low wall that was meant to keep the middle schoolers off the landscaping. She eyed him warily as she approached, trying to gauge if he was in one of his excitable moods that might lead him to forget she wasn't Naomi and launch himself at her or grab on to her arm. When Eitan only waved excitedly—like maybe he thought she had somehow missed his round buzzed head and neon orange backpack— and made no move toward her, she decided it was probably safe enough to approach. Eitan grinned at her and jumped off the wall, bouncing slightly on his toes until Becca was close enough to hear him over the chatter of the other students pushing and shoving their way into school.

"Did you get my text?" he demanded immediately.

"My parents got me a telescope because that lunar eclipse is happening the weekend after Hanukkah, and the second part of the present is a camping trip so we can go somewhere to see it really well! They let me open it early so you all would have time to plan! We *have* to camp that night, Becca. Did you ask your parents like I told you to?" He was still bouncing. "I texted this morning! Did you ask them?"

Becca had not, in fact, asked her parents if she could go camping with Eitan's family in a few weeks. It wasn't that she didn't want to go. Eclipses weren't really her thing, but she had been greedily studying all the star maps she could get her hands on since Jonah, Eitan's cousin who worked at the observatory, had given her a solar map last year on their adventure with the Golem. She'd pestered Eitan until he'd given her Jonah's phone number, and now one of her parents drove her out to the observatory twice a month so Jonah could go through his new data with her. It was pretty cool. Eitan's new telescope was basically a gift to Becca as well, since it meant she could study the stars on her own in between trips to the observatory. Still. "I didn't have time to ask my parents for anything," she told Eitan. "They're still fighting."

Eitan looked astonished. "But that was *yester-day!*"

"Some people's parents don't have years of couples therapy to fall back on, Eitan. They're not as good at conflict resolution." Becca huffed at Eitan's pinched expression and turned away from him, scanning the crowded parking lot. "Where's Nae?"

Eitan's face didn't quite unpinch, but he let her change the subject. "She's just running late. Deena's taking her to school today, and she never leaves on time." He shrugged. "Should we just meet her in first period?"

Becca grimaced. Deena always made them late to things when she was the one driving. It wasn't that unusual, but Becca wasn't prepared to have another interruption to her routine that morning. She glanced around. The crowds were thinning, but there was still a pretty sizable line of cars dropping kids off. "We have time," she decided. She led the way back to the low wall Eitan had been standing on before and sat down. Eitan trailed after her, darting glances at his watch. He seemed to finally decide that they did, in fact, have time, because he sat down next to her.

There was a slightly uncomfortable silence in which Eitan shifted a little nervously, and Becca ran back through their conversation in her head, trying to figure out what part had made Eitan quiet. He was only ever quiet when he was a little mad at her but didn't want to start a fight. They always tried not to fight when Naomi wasn't there to help them figure out what they were fighting about.

"Sorry," she tried.

Eitan darted a sideways glance at her. "Do you know which part you're saying sorry for?"

Becca huffed. "I'm not stupid."

That made Eitan sigh, but he smiled a little too. "You're not, Becks, but you also don't always catch what makes other people upset, you know?" He shrugged. "And I'm not as good at not getting upset at the things you say as Nae is. It's not anyone's fault."

Becca couldn't help but feel like maybe it was a little bit her fault. She ran through the conversation again. "It was the thing I said about your parents," she decided.

Eitan's smile was a little bigger now. "Yeah, it was. But I know you're upset about your parents too." He tilted sideways so he could bump shoulders with her. Becca let it happen. Eitan had been trying to be better about not touching her without permission, and it wasn't like he was hugging her.

"Sorry," she said again.

"What are we sorry for?" Becca and Eitan both jumped at the sound of Naomi's voice. Neither of them had noticed her walking up.

Eitan shook his head. "It's over, Nae," he said. "Don't worry about it." He hopped off the wall and threw his arm around Naomi, backpack, hood, big hair, and all, and nudged Becca's foot with his until she stood up too. "Walk and talk, ladies! We're going to be late!"

Naomi laughed and wrapped her arm around Eitan's waist, then held her hand out until Becca relented and shuffled close enough that Naomi could grab the hanging strap of her backpack to tow her along. "We're not going to be late!" Naomi said. "We've got five minutes until homeroom starts, and it's literally down the hall." She tugged on Becca's backpack strap. "Why were you sorry?"

"I said—"

"Becca's parents are still fighting!" Eitan cut in.

Naomi frowned. "Still? Well, it's only been a day.

I'm sure they'll figure it out." She nudged Becca. "I'm guessing that means you didn't ask if they would let you camp."

Becca shrugged. "I'm sure they will."

"Definitely," Naomi confirmed. "And I'm sure whatever they're fighting about will be over by the time your mom picks you up from school."

It wasn't over by the time Becca's mom picked her up from school. Jake and the twins were as rowdy and annoying in the back seat as usual, but their mom never once told them to quiet down. Not even when Ariela bit Jake and Jake hit her hard enough that Becca could hear it through her headphones. She turned around and pushed her siblings apart, sparing a sympathetic glance for Benji in the far back, who was trying to play a game on his Switch while tucked into a ball to avoid getting hit by flailing arms. Their mom didn't seem to notice the commotion, and she didn't even scold Jake for nearly making Ariela break her face on the pavement when he climbed over her to get out of the car. It wasn't until they got in the house, though, that Becca realized something was really wrong. Their father was home. He was *never* home earlier than seven at night from his job at the newspaper. They were always short-staffed, and something was always coming up that needed his attention as a managing editor. Becca looked at her mom, but her mom didn't seem surprised. She just sighed and nodded when Becca's father caught her eye.

"Jacob, Rebecca," she said, speaking for the first time since picking them up from school. Becca and Jake looked at each other, wide-eyed. Their mom never used their full names unless things were really serious. "We need to talk to you guys, okay?"

"Becca did it," Jake said immediately. "I had no idea."

Becca stuck her tongue out at him, but her dad cut her off before she could say anything back. "Neither of you is in trouble," he said. He sounded tired. "But this is important, okay? I need you guys to be serious." Becca nodded immediately, and Jake finally seemed to realize something was off. He shut his mouth and stopped trying to pull Becca off her feet by swinging from her backpack. Their father rubbed his hand down his face. "Okay, thank you. Let's talk in the living room."

Becca shuffled to the living room with her

brother and dropped down onto the couch. She felt prickly with tension, and she was hungry—she was supposed to use the bathroom and then have a snack when she got home from school; that was the way it went every day—and her skin was itchy in a way that felt a little too familiar and made her very, very nervous.

Her parents settled in the chairs across from them, still quiet in the distracted way Becca's mom had been in the car. Finally, her dad cleared his throat and leaned forward, resting his elbows on his knees.

"The paper is closing down," he said. "We don't have enough readers, and the owner is cutting his losses."

Becca tilted her head a little, trying to understand. Beside her, Jake was wearing an expression similar to the one he'd had when he caught a ball to the stomach during Little League practice. Her dad looked at them and nodded, like they had asked him a question out loud.

"That means I don't have a job anymore," he told them, "and until I can find another one, we're going to have to be a little more careful with our money."

"What does that mean?" Becca asked.

Her mom sighed. "It means we're going to have to cut back on the fun stuff for a while. Starting with Hanukkah."

"With *Hanukkah?*" Jake demanded. His eyes were giant in his face. It would have been funny if Becca weren't still trying to process what her parents were saying. "Are we not getting presents?"

"We'll have presents," her dad said, "but we're not going to do one every night, or anything big."

That was wrong. Hanukkah was supposed to be big. It was her mom's favorite holiday. They got small presents every night, so they always had something to open, and then something really big on the eighth night. That was how it was supposed to go. It was never as big as what Eitan or Naomi got—the newspaper didn't pay that much at the best of times, and her mom had tenure as a professor at the university, but it wasn't like she was a corporate lawyer—but it was always something. That was how things were *supposed* to go.

"We'll need you two to help set an example for the twins," Becca's dad was saying. "They're too little to really get it. So, please, just be good about this, okay?"

"Are we still going to visit Bubbe over break?"

Her mom sighed. "Probably not, Becca. It's a lot to pay for plane tickets for that many people."

"What about—"

Her dad's phone rang loudly, cutting her off. He rubbed his hands on his face again and pulled it out of his pocket. "I'm sorry, guys, I need to take this. Go get your snack. I'll answer any questions you have later."

Becca's mom nodded and stood up. She sent Jake to wash his hands again—there was always dirt under his nails—and kissed Becca on the top of the head. "Come eat so you can get to your homework, okay?"

Becca nodded but didn't get up to follow her mom. She felt like as long as she didn't move, things would stand still for a minute, but as soon as she stood up, everything would start shifting again. Her skin was crawling like her favorite sweater had suddenly turned scratchy and unfamiliar. There was no Golem around to blame for it this time, though, just bad news and worse changes. Becca really hated change.

2

SPIRITUALLY
GROWN-UPS

"And what does it mean to you to be a recognized adult in the Jewish community, now that you've all had a year to think about it?" Rabbi Levinson looked around the room. It was his day to lecture in their Hebrew school class—he dropped into every class once a quarter—and he wanted to talk about being grown-ups. Becca was tired of people talking to her about being grown-up. Rabbi Levinson spread his hands open like he was inviting the class inside somewhere. "Come on, you're all about to be high schoolers. You haven't noticed a change?"

"My allowance is higher," Jacob Katz joked from the corner. Becca rolled her eyes as his friends cheered and offered fist bumps.

Rabbi Levinson just smiled. "That's very exciting, Jacob. What extra responsibilities came with that?"

Jacob shrugged. "More chores, I guess, and helping my sister with her homework."

The rabbi nodded. "Very good. That's very helpful of you. Anyone else?"

The class was silent. Naomi was reading something on her phone under the table—it looked like a Supreme Court decision, actually, and Becca wasn't touching that with a ten-foot pole—and on her other side Eitan was scribbling notes into his class notebook. Becca was pretty sure he was writing down every word the rabbi said. Eitan loved the days Rabbi Levinson taught their class. Becca was embarrassed to know both of them.

"Well, let's see if anyone remembers our pre–B'nei Mitzvah classes," Rabbi Levinson was saying. "I'll ask you the same question I asked then. At thirteen, you can't vote, you can't drink, you can't buy anything you need to be an adult to buy, you can't even drive. L.A. County, California State, and the United States federal government have no policies that recognize B'nei Mitzvahs as a legal milestone. So, what does it mean that you're recognized as adults by our community?"

"It means no more Hanukkah presents," Becca muttered. Eitan's hand shot into the air so quickly Becca felt a breeze stir the loose pieces of hair around her face.

"It's about *spiritual* maturity," Eitan said.

The rabbi pointed at Eitan. "Indeed it is. And what does that mean?"

Eitan flipped through his notebook frantically. "Um, it means the ability to experience the depth and complexity of life," he read aloud. "With maturity comes the ability to sense subtlety and nuance. Our minds expand to be able to appreciate that even though something seems painful, there is a deeper good. And the things that feel good are not always good for us."

Becca rolled her eyes at Eitan's pleased, pink face.

Rabbi Levinson nodded seriously. "An excellent recap of the lecture, Eitan. Can anyone give me an example of what that means for them personally?"

There was some muttering and shuffling of

notebooks and feet—the kinds of sounds Becca knew that at school meant no one had done the reading. There wasn't any assigned Hebrew school reading, but it amounted to the same thing. The rabbi sighed. "Naomi," he said.

Naomi dropped her phone into her lap and snapped her head up. "Yes, Rabbi Levinson?" she said, making her eyes big and serious, like she could convince him she had been listening the whole time.

Rabbi Levinson pinched his lips together in a way that made Becca think he was probably try-ing not to smile. "Is everybody in prison the same level of bad?"

Naomi looked horrified, and Becca tried not to sigh. Rabbi Levinson should know better than to get Naomi started on these things. "No!" Naomi declared. "In fact, it's really unfair to say that everyone in prison is bad at all! Our prison system is biased against certain racial groups, and for-profit prisons are *totally* corrupt, and thousands of people are held for months or even years without a trial for tiny offenses. Plus, we're legalizing drugs that lots of people are in jail for right now, and we know that even if those drugs were still illegal, the war on drugs was created to target Black people and people who opposed the war in Vietnam, and those charges are always overblown, and—"

Becca reached out and pinched Naomi under the table. "Breathe," she whispered.

Rabbi Levinson was actually smiling now. "Indeed," he said. "What about the people who've killed other people? Do they deserve to be in our prison system?"

"Nobody deserves to be in our prison system," Naomi said darkly.

Rabbi Levinson tilted his head. "But they're bad."

"Prison reform has to include everyone, or it won't help anyone." Becca was pretty sure Naomi was quoting someone. "And most people don't hurt other people without their circumstances pushing them to make bad decisions."

"Ah," the rabbi said. "So we can't just say that some people are bad and deserve to be punished?"

Becca didn't think that sounded right. Some people *were* bad, she was pretty sure.

"Some people *are* bad," Naomi said, as if echoing Becca's thoughts. "But even bad people deserve to be treated humanely."

Rabbi Levinson pointed at Naomi like he had pointed at Eitan. "Spiritual maturity," he said. "Thank you for the example, Naomi. Now let's think about this on a smaller scale. Jacob." He turned to the other side of the classroom, and Naomi promptly pulled her phone back out.

Becca pinched her again. "One day you're going to get in trouble," she whispered.

It probably wasn't true. Ever since the Golem, Rabbi Levinson had kept an annoyingly close eye on the three of them when they were at the temple, but he had also been strangely more willing to let them get away with small things that would have gotten them in trouble before.

In his more paranoid moments, Eitan worried that the rabbi was waiting for the right time to expose them for everything. Becca had pointed out that the rabbi didn't necessarily know any-thing, but she had to admit that it was hard to explain away a giant Golem destroying the dam just a day or two after Becca and her friends had been in Rabbi Levinson's office asking him about how to stop Golems—not that the news had reported the Golem. It was explained away as an earthquake or something, but Rabbi Levinson had seemed like he didn't really believe it when he talked about the event. Not to mention the fact that the three of them had been unaccounted for during that time.

Rabbi Levinson had never said anything to their parents, though. He was cool. *And nice to look at*, Becca's traitorous brain supplied. She forced the thought down. That was a secret Becca could never share with Naomi, who was always talking about how gross it was that Deena and her friends thought Rabbi Levinson was cute. She couldn't know that Becca *agreed* with them. Though sometimes Becca thought Naomi was being a bit too defensive about the whole thing. It wasn't like she didn't have eyes. It didn't mean anything weird to admit that Rabbi Levinson had a good face.

She poked Naomi again for good measure, and Naomi slapped her hand away. Eitan shushed them.

"Jacob, when you help your sister with her homework," the rabbi was saying, "does she want to do it?"

Jacob snorted. "No."

The rabbi laughed. "And who can blame her? Does she put up a fight about it?"

"She whines the whole time," Jacob said. "It's so annoying."

"So, why do you make her do it?"

"*I* don't make her do it. I just help her. My *parents* make her do it."

"Fair enough," Rabbi Levinson said. "Why do you help her if it makes her so mad?"

"Because she's behind," Jacob said, "and she has to learn to *add* or she'll have to repeat second grade."

"Aha. So something that seems painful but contains a deeper good. Your sister is too young to realize that, but you, Jacob, have the *spiritual maturity* to understand that sometimes the world isn't so black or white."

Jacob shrugged. "I guess."

"You guess right!" Rabbi Levinson exclaimed. There were some giggles from the class at that, but they quieted as the rabbi continued. "Your B'nei Mitzvahs symbolize that your community recognizes you're old enough to see those shades of gray we've been talking about. You are adults in the sense that the childhood belief that things can be divided easily into right and wrong, true and false, or good and bad is behind you now."

He clapped his hands together. "Congratulations! You're spiritually grown-ups!"

"Okay, but some things are just true," Becca said. They were waiting outside the temple for their parents, and Naomi had finished her rant on the court opinion she had been reading in class, and Becca couldn't hold in her confusion anymore. "Rabbi Levinson made this huge deal about how nothing is black or white, or whatever, but there are some things that *are*. Like, scientifically."

"I don't think he really meant scientific facts, Becks," Naomi said gently. "More like questions of morality and judgment."

"Okay," Becca repeated, "but sometimes those things are just true, too. You say so all the time!"

Naomi bit her lip a little, like she was thinking of the best way to explain something simple to Becca. Becca hated that look. It made her feel small and silly, like Naomi was her big sister teaching her basic things, instead of being practically the same age. When they were little, Becca used to get so frustrated with not knowing things that everyone around her seemed to just *understand* that she would stop talking for days at a time. She didn't do that anymore, but her parents were fighting, and her Hanukkah was *ruined*, and things were changing, and Naomi was standing there with that patient thinking face like Becca was a *baby*, and Becca just wanted to stop thinking about how to be a grown-up for a few minutes. She clenched her fists tightly against the urge to drag her hands up and down her arms to settle herself. It didn't work. She gave in, rubbing her arms through her sweatshirt like she could rub away the feeling of *wrong*ness that had settled into her skin ever since her parents had started yelling at each other where Becca could hear it.

Naomi's face changed from her patient thinking one to a much more worried expression. "Oh, Becks, it's okay." She took off her own jacket and wrapped it around Becca tightly. Eitan added his on top of hers, and Becca gathered both in one fist, grateful for the extra weight and pressure.

"We don't have to talk about this now," Naomi said quietly. "And it's not like Rabbi Levinson said we all have to get it right away. Everyone learns and grows at different paces."

"Well, I'm tired of being behind," Becca said.

She couldn't bring herself to look away from the ground, so she wasn't sure what Naomi's face was doing now.

Naomi sighed. "You're not behind, Becks. Everyone has different strengths. It's not a bad thing that you see things super clearly all the time. You know I need that sometimes when I get all tangled up in my head. And we'll help you when we need a different approach, right, Eitan?"

"Right," Eitan agreed.

"See?"

Becca shrugged. It sounded good when Naomi said it, but she still felt like maybe there was something she was missing. She didn't get a lot of time to think about it, though, because her mom pulled up in front of the temple, and Becca had to help collect all her siblings from their Hebrew school teachers. Then she had to go get an extra cupcake from the second-grade classroom to make sure Jake got his own so he wouldn't steal Ariela's. And *then* Benji threw up on the driveway at home because the cupcakes had buttercream and he really wasn't supposed to have dairy, but her mom had already run inside to take a call on her office phone, and her dad was away packing up his office at the newspaper, so Becca had to clean Benji up and hose off the driveway. When she finally got back inside, Jake had made both twins cry by changing the channel from their usual after-school shows to something violent that he probably wasn't supposed to be watching and *definitely* wasn't supposed to be playing around the twins.

Becca wrestled the remote away from him and put the twins' educational show back on. She dragged Jake to the bathroom and threatened to lock him inside until he showered, then hovered outside until she heard the water actually turn on and Jake start the obnoxious rapping that meant he'd found a spot with good acoustics and a bar of soap to pretend was a microphone. Then she went downstairs to do her homework until one of her siblings started shrieking again and she had to get up and corral them all over again. Being grown-up, she decided, was not at all worth it.

3

A FLIPPED PERSPECTIVE

The week kept getting worse after that. Jake took it in turns being mopey and snappish at their parents. Especially once he found out he wouldn't be able to do Little League in the spring unless their father was able to find a new job very quickly or the team let him apply as a scholarship player. He had outgrown all his equipment from last year, and there just wasn't a way to pay for new gear at the moment. Becca was sympathetic. She would have been beyond upset if she had to quit softball. It was pure luck, she knew, that her team supplied the gear. Jake was angry about this, too, and had taken to hiding her stuff around the house where he knew it wasn't supposed to go. It was unusually mean, even for Jake. Her brother's behavior also meant that the instruction to "set a good example for the twins" fell to Becca alone.

"It's just not fair," she complained, sprawled on a blanket on the grass in the Teitelbaums' backyard as Naomi fussed over her compost bins. It was nice to be able to say it quietly, like a secret. Normally, Eitan would insist on being so far away from the bins that Becca would have to raise her voice to make sure Naomi could hear her. He swore the bins smelled when Naomi opened them. Becca thought that was rich coming from a boy who had discovered spray-on deodorant three months ago and had only agreed to cut back on his use of it when Becca refused to carpool with him until he did. Naomi had backed her up, pointing out that aerosols were bad for the environment on top of stinking up the place. The compost bins did have a smell, but unlike Eitan's questionable body spray, it was a natural, earthy smell that didn't stick out from the other smells of the backyard.

"What's not fair?" Naomi asked. "I think my worms are cold. What do you think, Becks? Should

I get them a heating light? No, that's expensive and we'd need an extension cord. I could probably just wrap them in blankets, right?"

"It's L.A." Becca huffed. "It's never below, like, forty-five degrees."

"Worms do best at fifty-seven degrees and warmer," Naomi recited. "Any lower than that and they start to die." She tapped her chin a few times, then seemed to remember that Becca had said something. "What's not fair, Becks?"

"That I have to listen to you talk about worms when I'm in crisis," Becca retorted.

Naomi pursed her lips and went to sit on the blanket with Becca. "Sorry," she said. "Really, what's not fair?"

Becca sighed. "Mom and Dad talked to me *and* Jake. Why does Jake get to be terrible about it and I have to be totally good and nice so the twins don't start acting terrible, too?"

Naomi shrugged a little. "Jake's always terrible, Becks. What did you expect?"

Becca rolled her eyes. She should have known that Naomi wouldn't get it. She was the youngest. She didn't have to set an example for anyone. At least she was still a little better than Eitan, who was an only child and therefore definitely couldn't understand the horribleness of siblings.

"Okay," Becca said, "but they specifically asked him *not* to be terrible this time. And honestly, I should get to be a little terrible about it, too, right? Because I'm going to for sure get the smallest Hanukkah present since I'm the oldest, and we're not going to visit Bubbe anymore even though she *promised* she's been buying all the good maps from the estate sales in her neighborhood." Becca felt hot tears pricking at the corners of her eyes and scrubbed at them. She was basically a grown-up now, she reminded herself. It was stupid to cry about Hanukkah presents. "So what, I'm *spiritually mature*, and Jake just . . . gets to act like a baby?"

"Oh, Becks, is that still bothering you?" Naomi asked, settling a little closer on the blanket but not so close that Becca felt stifled. "You can cry, you know. Mama cries all the time. She says it's cleansing for the soul." She leaned in, like she was sharing a secret. "Sometimes I think she cries on purpose so she can be extra cleansed."

Becca snorted. "I don't think that's how it works, but thanks." She slumped over, allowing

Naomi's knee to press against her leg. "Home is just so uncomfortable all the time now. I'm *itchy* all over whenever I'm there."

Naomi's eyes went wide. "Itchy how?" she demanded.

Becca shivered at the memory. "Not like *that,*" she said. "But . . . also not *not* like that," she added.

Naomi squinted at her. "What does that mean?"

"It means that it feels the same as last year, but it can't be, because you buried the last three Golems you got in the yard!" They both looked toward the abandoned little garden patch behind the compost bins. Naomi's mom had once had the idea that gardening would help with the stress of her work at the DA's office, but she hadn't actually liked doing it, and Naomi's mama always said she had a brown thumb, whatever that meant. So the garden stayed a patch of dirt, and then, more recently, became a makeshift graveyard for unactivated Golems. Naomi had received two more packages containing little clay figures and unsigned scrolls since she had refused to wake up the one that had appeared at her Bat Mitzvah reception. She buried them all and marked the spots with smooth, round stones they stole from Eitan's front yard. Eitan called it her pet cemetery, but Becca knew he was way too much of a scaredy-cat to actually know what that story was about. It was weird—not to mention more than a little scary—that they kept showing up, but Naomi also never woke them, which meant there was nothing to cause Becca's crawling skin besides her usual discomfort in her own body. She said as much to Naomi, who let out a long breath.

"Well," she said slowly, "it wasn't just the Golems that made that happen, though. There were lots of other things, too."

"Yeah, but there were Golems first."

"You could say there are still Golems," Naomi pointed out.

"Okay, fine, it is weird that they keep show-ing up. That's why we put Eitan on the case. But they're not *awake*. Last time the itchy magic didn't start until the Golem was awake."

Naomi shook her head. "I don't know, Becks. We don't actually know anything about the magic. The Golem started it, but . . ." She trailed off, staring toward the neat row of stones in the garden patch. "I'm just saying, we should be a little careful. It's been almost a year since we felt anything, but that doesn't mean there's nothing out there."

"There's nothing out there," Becca said firmly. "I'm having a physical response to an emotional situation. It's not unprecedented, Nae."

"I guess." Her friend still had the scrunched-up expression on her face that Becca had learned meant she was feeling doubtful about a situation.

Becca reached into her pocket for her worry stone, pinching the cold, polished rock between her fingers while she thought. "I'll keep an eye out," she offered, "and maybe we can tell Eitan, too, just so he can keep an eye out for . . . I don't know . . . monsters that are summoned by extra-sad Hanukkahs or something."

Naomi's face immediately smoothed out. "Perfect!" she said. "I'm texting him now."

"Whatever." Becca ran her thumb over the shallow indentation in her worry stone. "I'm telling you, there's nothing magical happening in my house."

Becca lingered at the Teitelbaum house as long as she could, but Naomi had tech week for a theater club show starting up, and her moms always made her go to bed early the whole week before since the rehearsals went so late into the night—so

Becca eventually had to take her bike and make her way home. The house was still full of the weird, tense energy that felt like it had been oozing out of the walls since that first day Becca had come home to find her dad already there. Her parents weren't fighting anymore, but they weren't really talking to each other, either, and only sort of talking to Becca and her siblings. In the week since her parents had shared the news, Becca had taken over walking the twins through their first-grade homework and reading them their bedtime stories while her dad took phone call after phone call in his office and her mom sent a million emails on her computer asking anyone she knew about job leads for journalists.

There was no one in the kitchen when Becca stuck her head around the corner. Her mom had gone out for some faculty social event, but she could hear Jake in his room, yelling at his video game, and shrieking from the bathroom that meant the twins were being forced to shower, which answered the question of where her dad was. Becca let out a small breath of relief that she wouldn't need to talk to anyone for a little while and then shivered as goose bumps rose along her arms and the back of her neck, making her skin feel tight and itchy.

"A physical response to an emotional situation," Becca muttered to herself. "There's no magic here."

She repeated the words to herself as she made her way down the hall to her room and flipped the light switch. "There's no magic—"

Her room had been turned upside down. Literally. Everything in her room was exactly where it should have been, but all of it was upside down. The drawers that went under her bed were stacked neatly on top of the bed frame, which was stacked neatly on top of the still-made mattress. Becca could see the corner of her pillow sticking out from under the whole thing. Her books sat in the right order—color and size—on her bookshelf, the legs of which brushed the ceiling. Her desk, her dresser, her shoe stand, even her clothes somehow stood perfectly vertically up from the closet rod stretched across the carpet. Becca shut the door behind her and walked slowly over to the closet and pushed at a shirt. The material rippled and then settled straight again like it really was hanging. Becca rubbed at her arms and then at her ears as tiny voices started whispering and giggling just at the edge of her hearing. Something small and unseen *whooshed* by, rustling her clothes and making the hems of her pants flap against her ankles.

Becca scrambled to get out of the way. Her back collided with the wall, and she slid down it into a crouch. The thing continued to zip around the room, like it didn't realize Becca was there. She wrapped her arms around her knees, trying to think over the sound of her heart pounding in her ears and the feeling of ants crawling over her skin. Something bounced off Becca's ankle with a tiny warbling hiss, and she could see the small dent in the carpet where it had hit the ground before zooming away again. Becca narrowed her eyes, watching the long fibers of her carpet sway as the thing sped back and forth around her room. It upended her trash can, somehow keeping all the crumpled paper perfectly underneath the wire basket, and in the next breath was on the other side of the room, flipping her lamp onto its head. It slammed into the door a few times as well, but didn't seem able to open it. That was strange for a creature that could rearrange her entire room without her family noticing, but Becca wasn't feeling like figuring out that particular logic puzzle at the moment.

She inched sideways toward her gym bag—still

hanging from its hook, suspended upside down in the air—and slowly unzipped it, letting the contents fall to the ground until she found what she was looking for. She slipped her mitt onto her hand and dropped into a crouch, trying to track the path of the little monster by the way the carpet moved. It was harder than catching a gnat, but Becca watched it carefully, noticing which small things in her room still hadn't been flipped. Then the thing zipped under her bed and emerged with, of all things, a yellow plastic dreidel. It must have rolled there when she was playing with the twins in her room the other day. They had come home from someone's Hanukkah party earlier that week clutching bags of chocolate coins and two plastic dreidels each.

Becca still couldn't see whatever it was that was making the mess, but it didn't seem to want to let go of the dreidel, which made it a lot easier to follow. It zipped around in a gleeful yellow blur, flipping into the air when the thing stopped to turn something over and then zipping on to the next. Becca looked around her room, her mitt still clutched in her hand. There. She slid on her knees over to her night-light. It was still in its proper place, and the soft halo of cool light projecting from the purple crystal on its little stand cast a small shadow on the pale carpet. Becca sat to the side of it and waited. Then her hand shot out, and there was a tiny outraged "oof" as she clapped her other hand over the mitt to hold the thing inside. Something sharp lanced across her palm, and she hissed but didn't let go.

There was a jar on her desk that usually held pens, but it had been emptied that morning in Benji's search for more colors. Becca had been furious at the time. She told herself she would apologize to Benji later as she took hold of the invisible wriggling form of whatever creature she had just caught and thrust it into the jar, dreidel and all, then slammed the lid over it, screwing it tightly shut. She let go and stared at it. For a moment, it gave a very good impression of a yellow plastic dreidel in a jar, and then the dreidel started to spin. The glass shuddered against the tabletop, and Becca winced as something sharp dragged down the wall of the container. The sound reminded her of her stinging hand, and she looked down, frowning at the shallow cut that stretched across her palm. It needed to be disinfected. That was the first priority. Becca didn't want to think about the number of weird germs a magical creature might have under its nails, if it even was its nail that Becca had been scratched by. She swallowed the gagging feeling of grossness that threatened to derail her whole train of thought and forced herself to focus. First aid, then reinforcements. A plan.

Becca managed to get her hand clean and wrapped without her dad noticing she was digging through the family first aid kit—Becca had never been so grateful that her twin siblings were such a handful—and made her way back to her room. The jar was where she had left it. It still looked empty, but every couple of seconds it shook like something inside was testing the strength of the glass. Reinforcements. Becca pulled out her phone and started a video call to the group. Eitan answered at once.

"I thought you guys needed 'girl time,'" he said immediately, putting such exaggerated quotes around the words that Becca could tell right away he was being sarcastic.

"You said you were having a guys' night with Troy," Becca reminded him. "You said, verbatim, that you 'had to hang out with friends who didn't expect you to be so smart all the time,' and that we should 'do girl stuff, or whatever.'"

Eitan rolled his eyes. "Your memory is so freaky sometimes, Becks," he said. "And Troy's wasn't any fun anyway. He never wants to talk about anything interesting." Eitan sighed. "Anyway, what's up?"

"Hello? Are you okay?" Naomi's voice as she joined the call was quiet, and her screen was dark. Tech week, Becca remembered. Naomi was in bed already.

"Sorry, Nae, it's just—" Becca flipped the phone camera so she could show them her room, then zoomed in on the still-shaking jar on her desk.

Eitan said a word they were definitely not allowed to use, and Naomi shrieked loudly, then shushed herself.

"Yeah," Becca agreed. "So, remember how I said there was nothing magical in my house? I think maybe I was wrong about that."

4

SMALL IMP,
BIG PROBLEMS

"We're not even supposed to be here!"

Becca shushed Eitan, swatting at him with her free hand while she punched in the door code Naomi had given them. "We go to school here," she reminded Eitan. The door chimed, and she pulled it open, gesturing for Eitan to be quiet. Predictably, he didn't listen.

"Not at night!" Eitan insisted. He followed her inside, though, still far too close and agitated for Becca to be able to concentrate properly on not tripping in the dark hallway. "And never in the theater building! We're barely allowed in this part of the school during daylight!"

"You're panicking," Becca told him. The anxious press of Eitan's words—too fast and too forceful—was grating on Becca's already raw nerves. She wasn't usually so affected by Eitan's anxiety, but her skin was also crawling from having the invisible creature in her backpack for so long. She felt like her whole body was one exposed wire. "It's fine." She meant it both for Eitan and for herself. "If we get caught, we just tell them we came to drop something off for Naomi and got lost."

"You want to *lie*?" Eitan said disbelievingly. *"You?"*

"It's not a lie," Becca said. "We really are here to bring Naomi something. There." She pointed at the paper sign taped to a door at the end of the hall indicating that the bathroom had been converted into the girls' dressing room for the week. It had clearly been made by a student; Becca didn't think the theater teachers were printing tech week signs in horror movie font. There were lights down that way, too, which helped Eitan calm down, which in turn helped Becca focus on where she was going. Naomi had given them very specific instructions, and Eitan was right about the fact that the two of them didn't spend very much time in the maze of soundproofed practice rooms and costume and set storage that was the theater and arts building.

"I just want you to know," Eitan whispered at her as she pulled him through the halls, counting room numbers, "that I am not *panicking*. I am expressing perfectly reasonable concerns about being in trouble. Do *you* want to go to jail for trespassing, Becks? *I'm* not trying to go to jail for trespassing. *I'm* trying to get into Stanford!"

"You're thirteen," Becca reminded him. "No one's going to arrest you *or* let you into Stanford."

"It'll go on our record! And then they'll never let me into Stanford, even when I'm old enough to go!"

"Why do you even want to go there? We have perfectly good schools around here."

"The universe is bigger than the Valley, Becks," Eitan said loftily, sufficiently distracted from the prospect of getting caught by the chance to be superior about academics. "Sometimes you need to leave your bubble to really learn anything."

"And go *all the way* to the Bay Area," Becca said flatly, still scanning rooms. Eitan sputtered at her, but he didn't get to answer because "Here!" Becca said triumphantly. The door to room 440 was locked, but there was light shining through the crack at the bottom. Becca rapped their secret code against the wood of the door, and it swung open.

"Finally!" Naomi hissed, pulling them inside. "You guys took forever! I have to be onstage in, like, twenty minutes! What happened?"

"Eitan was panicking," Becca said primly.

"Shut up," Eitan snapped.

"Guys! Time crunch!" Naomi held out an expectant hand. Becca shrugged out of her backpack and pulled out the jar, passing it to Naomi. The yellow dreidel rattled around the bottom, but nothing else seemed to be in there. Naomi turned it around in front of her face a few times. Then she set it on the table, and the three of them gathered around it. Eitan pulled out his phone and shone a light through the jar.

"Watch," Becca said. She tapped firmly on the glass of the jar three times. The dreidel stood on end, and then the jar tapped back. Eitan scrambled even closer, staring keenly at the jar. Becca had refused to show it to him until they found Naomi, and he had been pouting all evening.

"Do it again," he said.

Becca tapped the jar again. There was a long moment of silence, and then the jar rattled violently on the desk and let out a sound like an angry teakettle. "Okay," Eitan said. "Okay. Okay." He scrubbed both hands over his hair. "Okay." Becca reached out without looking and pinched his arm. "Right, sorry," Eitan said. He looked like maybe he was going to say something else, then thought better of it and turned toward the girls. "Nae?"

Naomi was looking thoughtfully at the jar. "Why can't we see it?" she asked.

"I don't know," Becca said. "It's definitely there, though, and it is a *thing*." She waved her hand. "Not like . . . just incorporeal"—this was a word she had learned from Jonah—"or whatever. It scratched me." She showed them her bandaged palm as evidence.

"Ew," Naomi said.

Eitan leaned in close to peer at the gauze around Becca's hand like it would give him some insight into the type of creature that had hurt her. Becca hissed at him when he reached out to touch it. Eitan took a step back and held up his hands, scowling at her.

"So, how do we make it visible?" Naomi asked, ignoring their exchange.

Becca shrugged. "How should I know?"

Naomi turned her thoughtful look on Becca, tapping her chin like she did when she was about to say something crazy, which was often. Sure enough: "You made that fake tree disappear. The one in the loop with the stretchy-armed demons."

"I remember," Becca said cautiously. Those demons had been particularly scary. Becca wasn't about to forget them anytime soon.

Naomi nodded encouragingly, like this train of thought made any logical sense. "So, how did you do it?"

Becca shrugged again. "I don't know. I just knew what was *supposed* to be there."

"So the illusion disappeared because you didn't believe in it."

Just like that, Becca understood what her friend was getting at. It sounded very simple when Naomi said it, but this felt more complicated. Becca trusted her maps, and they had told her that the tree was wrong. She wasn't sure what she was supposed to trust now. "So what?"

"So do it again."

Becca huffed in frustration. "Do what again? Not believe in the thing that is clearly in that jar?"

"Believe in what's real! Make what's supposed to be here show up! You're super certain of things, right? So be certain of this!"

"I don't *know* what's supposed to be there!"

"Here!" Eitan shouldered his way between them, holding up a picture on his phone of a familiar book.

Becca and Naomi stared at him for a moment before Naomi snorted and tapped on the phone. The image changed, and Becca realized it was an ebook. Naomi swiped a few more pages and then grinned at Becca. "Well, that's one theory."

Becca rolled her eyes and shoved Eitan back from where he was trying to push the phone into her face like she couldn't already see it. "Absolutely not," she said. "I do not have *Hanukkah goblins*."

Eitan swayed into Naomi's space, and she caught him easily with an arm around his waist. "Why not?" he asked. "It's Hanukkah. You have a mean invisible creature small enough to fit in a jar turning your room upside down. It literally stole your dreidel." He made an awkward motion that was probably meant to be a shrug, but he couldn't really move his shoulders properly with the way he was leaning against Naomi. "Who's to say that's not what it is?"

"That's not how anything works!" Becca insisted.

"We don't really know how anything works," Naomi reminded her. "We just know what worked for us before." She released Eitan and stepped back, sticking her tongue out at him when he stumbled backward with a squawk. "It doesn't hurt to try. Plus, I only have like"—she checked her watch—"fifteen minutes left. So moves have got to be made."

"Go on, Becks," Eitan encouraged her.

Becca sighed. She wasn't sure what she had expected to happen when she brought the jar to her friends, but it wasn't them making her do this all by herself. *Jake wasn't supposed to leave me by myself to be responsible either*, she thought moodily. *It's going around.* But that wasn't fair. Naomi and Eitan weren't abandoning her. They believed in her. She was always trying to convince people to believe in her. She just wished that maybe they didn't believe in her quite so much just then. *You're basically a grown-up*, she reminded herself. *Doing things by yourself is just part of it.*

"Becks?" Eitan prompted. Becca realized she'd been quiet for longer than was probably normal.

"Yeah," she said. "All right, why not? Show me the picture." Eitan flipped back through the book on his phone until he found an illustration of the smallest goblin and held it up. Becca peered at it, feeling more than a little ridiculous. At least it was something to focus on, though she wasn't sure what she would have done if they had told her to just *imagine* a goblin. Naomi was the one who did the imagining—sometimes so much that she upset herself with things that hadn't actually happened. Becca kept trying to explain to her that that was a nonsensical thing to do, but Naomi never seemed to quite get it. A picture was good. Becca could hold a picture in her head.

She closed her eyes for a second, trying to remember what she had done with the fake tree by the campground. It was hard to replicate. Then, she had simply been sure the tree was *wrong*. Becca wasn't so sure that the tiny invisible creature was meant to be a visible goblin.

"Ten minutes, Becks," Naomi whispered.

"Don't rush me!" Becca hissed back. She looked at the goblin picture again, then over at the empty jar. "Okay," she told it, "things with mass aren't meant to be invisible. That's not how anything works. You can be translucent but not *invisible*. Which means that this is a trick." She was aware of Naomi and Eitan watching her curiously, but she tried to focus only on the jar in front of her. "It's a trick," she repeated. "You aren't actually invisible. Look the way you're supposed to." She mustered up as much determination as she could, narrowing her eyes at the jar and trying to remember the feeling of certainty she'd had when she walked through the tree. *"Look the way you're supposed to."*

There was a blur in the jar that made Becca blink and then a popping noise like a suction cup pulling off a window. Then, between one blink and the next, the jar wasn't empty anymore.

"Holy smokes," she whispered.

"Yeah," Naomi agreed. "Great job, Becca."

Becca shot her a quick smile, then shifted her attention back to the jar almost immediately. Eitan had leaned in to take a bunch of photos on his phone as soon as the tiny creature had appeared. Becca kicked the side of his foot until he moved over enough that she could get a good look at the jar. The goblin looked similar to the picture in that it was small and kind of pointy and greenish, but that was where the similarities ended. The goblin pulled grotesque faces and twisted its limbs—and Becca wasn't totally sure exactly how many limbs it had—into shapes that anything with a functioning skeletal system probably shouldn't be able to make. It chittered at them in a voice almost too high to hear and dragged the spiny bits of its body down the glass sides of the jar to make a screeching noise that set Becca's teeth on edge. It was also clutching the bright yellow dreidel tightly to itself, which made it a lot less intimidating.

"Hey!" she shouted. The thing in the jar hissed at her but stopped scraping the glass. "Are you a goblin?" she asked it.

The creature made a wet gurgling sound that could have meant anything, though Becca thought it wasn't meant to be very nice. "I am *not* a *goblin*," it said in a voice like an industrial sander had been sucking helium. Becca startled. She hadn't really expected it to talk. "I am one of the mazzikim," it went on. "A destroyer."

Naomi snorted, and Becca and Eitan turned to

look at her. "Sorry," she said. "He's just so tiny."

"He managed to turn everything in my room upside down," Becca reminded her.

Naomi still looked like she was trying not to laugh. "Sure. But he's not exactly a strike-fear-into-the-hearts-of-men type."

The creature gurgled again, and Eitan turned to look at it. "Okay, so what's the singular for mazzikim? Is it mazzik?"

"Why is that important?" Becca demanded.

Eitan shrugged. "Well, we can't just keep calling it 'one of the mazzikim.'"

"A *destroyer*," Naomi put in. She was definitely giggling now. Becca glared at her, and the not-a-goblin-maybe-a-mazzik howled in fury and started to scratch at the glass again. Becca winced and tried shouting again, but it kept shrieking and scraping its claws down the walls of the jar until she could barely hear herself think.

The three of them stared at it, dumbstruck, until Naomi's phone buzzed loudly on the table-top. She yelped. "Oh my gosh, guys, that's curtain. I have to go. I'm sorry! You can deal with the *destroyer*, right? I totally believe in you!" She scrubbed a hand over Eitan's hair, blew Becca a kiss, and dashed out of the room with one last cry of, "Text me!" Then she was gone, and Eitan and Becca were alone with the creature.

"Well," Eitan said, "what now?"

5

YOU AND I ARE
SURELY FIVE

Something shifted in the room after Naomi left.
With all three of them there, the goblin—the
mazzik, Becca corrected in her head—had been
loud and full of rage. It seemed to be making
noise simply to be as unpleasant as possible,
which had worked: Becca could feel the sounds
like the demon was scratching its sharp little
limbs over her too-tight skin rather than down the
sides of the jar. Then Naomi left, and the creature
was abruptly quiet. It regarded them thoughtfully for a moment, its contorted motions slowing
enough that Becca could pick out three bulbous,

red-tinged eyes behind the swaying green limbs.

A crackling, staticky noise burbled out of the creature, different from the gurgling but just as malicious. After a moment Becca realized it was *laughing*. She shuddered. Beside her, she felt Eitan do the same. The creature kept laughing until it felt like the whole room was buzzing with the high-pitched noise. Then it stopped abruptly and pressed its protruding eyes against the glass of the jar.

"Two," it said, "is a very unlucky number."

"What?" Becca said.

"Three was fine, but now there's two, and that just spells bad luck for you," the goblin singsonged.

Becca wrinkled her forehead. "Are you *rhyming*? What are you even going to do if we're an unlucky number? You're in a jar."

The mazzik just laughed again. The sound of it made Becca shudder, and the goose bumps on her arms got even worse. She *hated* being around magic.

"Bad luck, bad luck," the demon was muttering.

Becca looked at Eitan. "What's happening here?"

Eitan shook his head, but it wasn't really a no. He had a deep wrinkle between his eyebrows, and he had sucked his bottom lip all the way into his mouth. When he shook his head while he was making that face, it meant he was thinking hard and needed a minute. Becca shut her mouth, waiting for whatever it was that Eitan was coming up with.

Finally, Eitan looked back at her. The wrinkle in his forehead was still there, but he'd let his lip go, which meant he was ready to tell her something. "I think I remember this," he said. "It's not much. It was just a silly passage my dad read to me once. His temple study group is doing Daf Yomi, remember?"

Becca didn't, really. She tried to think back to the last time she'd had dinner at Eitan's house and what his dad had been talking about. It was hard with the mazzik still laughing in the background. "That thing where they study one page of the Talmud every day for, like, seven years or something?"

"Yeah."

"Oh . . . *kay*. So, what did it say?"

Eitan shook his head again. "It was talking about even numbers being dangerous and how demons could harm you because of them if you weren't careful. But it was about *drinking*. Like don't drink in pairs or something." He jerked his head toward the demon. "I don't know why it's saying we're unlucky just standing here."

Becca shrugged. "Maybe it didn't have a good study group."

Eitan snorted. "Please be serious." He glanced nervously at the little creature in the jar, still pressing its eyes to the glass and muttering about bad luck.

"I'm serious," Becca said. "Maybe it's more about what the demons *think* will let them cause harm."

Eitan looked surprised, then thoughtful. "Okay, that's a really interesting thought and has just wild implications for—"

"Eitan." Becca didn't actually know what the word implications meant, but she knew what it sounded like when Eitan was about to get lost in a thought spiral. "How do you fix the pairs situation?" She hesitated. "Does one of us leave?"

"No." He stopped, looking a little red. Becca huffed. They really didn't have time for Eitan to feel embarrassed just then.

"*What*, Eitan?"

"We have to get it to count to one hundred and

one," he said. "In the story, once they counted that high, the demon got so mad he exploded."

"Get it to count?" Becca echoed. "That's it?"

Eitan shrugged. "Worth a shot, right?" He turned back to the goblin in the jar and took a breath. His hands were fidgety, and he cleared his throat a few times, but finally he started talking. "Bad luck may be, but not for me. You and me and she make three."

"Why are *you* rhyming now?" Becca demanded. "Is that part of it?"

Eitan shushed her, though his face had gotten even more red. The mazzik had stopped muttering and was looking at them thoughtfully. It wasn't laughing anymore either.

"Holy smokes," Becca muttered. "All right, fine. Rhyming it is."

The demon hissed and brandished the yellow dreidel. "Three you say, and not one more? She, he, me, and the dreidel is four."

"The dreidel?" Becca wasn't sure what was happening. "How does the dreidel count?"

Eitan shrugged. "Demon rules," he reminded her. "Better find one hundred and one things to count, I guess."

"There aren't one hundred and one unique things in the room," Becca told him.

"Figure it out, Becks," Eitan said. "Unless you want to do the rhymes?"

Becca groaned in annoyance and turned her back on her friend, scouring the room for countable items.

Eitan cleared his throat again and announced, "We're not out yet. We're still alive. We three, the dreidel, and the table make five."

The mazzik growled and hissed, running its spiny limbs down the glass again and making Becca shudder. "I'm wise to you and your little tricks. Those four, the table, and the jar is six."

The room was full of things—it was one of the classrooms set aside for overflow theater props and spare art supplies—but Becca wasn't sure whether Eitan could repeat anything. Somehow, she didn't think counting out one hundred and one colored pencils would work within whatever set of rules the tiny demon was using. She started pulling one of everything: a piece of colored paper, a jar of paint, a bolt of fabric, and anything else she could find that wasn't nailed down and piling it up in front of Eitan. She kept half an ear on the rhyming battle—*poetry slam*, she thought a little hysterically, remembering Deena's phase of ambushing the three of them with videos of people doing spoken word poetry to "educate them in the arts."

Eitan seemed to be holding his own, though some of his rhymes were frankly a little ridiculous. Becca wasn't sure she was going to be able to let him live down the number of syllables he fumbled trying to fit *eleven* into a rhyming sentence or trying to make *curtain* rhyme with *thirteen*. Still, it was working. The mazzik was counting higher and higher and getting more and more frustrated as they went. It had stopped dragging its spines down the glass and instead had set the glass humming at a whining, high-pitched frequency that did nothing for Becca's already-jangling nerves.

It was also difficult to keep track of the exact count of the items she was pulling out, with the mazzik and Eitan rhyming numbers in the background. It was too much sensory input. The only positive was that Becca was now so agitated she couldn't tell if her skin was crawling because of the magic or because of everything else. She scrubbed uselessly at her arms, bouncing on her toes as she looked around for something she might have missed. There was a tower of art supplies in front of Eitan, and he was picking them up one at a time as his turn to count came up, but—and Becca felt silly that she hadn't thought of this—the goblin was *also* choosing items from the pile. It was cutting the amount of useful things she'd found in half.

A look through the battered file cabinet on the far wall of the classroom yielded a broken key chain, an old pack of gum, and a rubber band ball. The drawers under the counter held a mini three-hole-punch and a plastic magnifying glass. Becca gathered them all up in her sweatshirt pocket and scurried over to add them to the pile.

"Not out of luck yet. It'll all be fine. All that plus a . . . tail-less Charizard toy? Is eighty-nine?"

Becca snorted a little at Eitan's dubious tone. Some of the stuff was weird, but it wasn't Becca's job to preserve Eitan's dignity. It was her job to find more than one hundred unique items in a rarely used public school classroom. She fished a stapler out from under a shelf and found a book that was being used to prop up a wobbly desk and brought those to Eitan as well. Then she started to get desperate. The pile had shrunk to almost nothing, and Eitan and the mazzik still had twelve numbers to get through. Becca hurried back to Eitan's side. She shifted from one foot to the other, trying to think, but nothing was coming to her. It all seemed very silly. The demon was in the jar, and there wasn't anything high stakes about counting random things in a classroom, but something about the situation made Becca very sure that things would suddenly get a lot more dangerous for them if they lost this counting game. Eitan was stressed, too. Becca could tell because he was chewing his thumbnail during the goblin's turns. His mom had dipped his thumbs in spicy mustard for weeks to break him of that habit. He never even looked at his nails anymore unless something was making him very, very nervous. Becca saw Eitan shoot a scrunched-up look at the spread of stuff on the floor and knew she was right. Eitan had clearly also realized that they didn't have enough stuff to get them all the way to one hundred and one.

"For good luck, there's still some time. Add this ball"—Eitan held up an orange stress ball with large gray dents in it where chunks of foam had been torn out—"we're ninety-nine."

He was speaking super slowly now, and Becca

realized he was trying to buy her time. She spun in circles, looking for anything she might have missed. The mazzik cackled and made the jar wobble dangerously on the table. Then he pointed to a single stray paper clip on the floor, the last thing left in Becca's pile.

"You're out of things and should have fled. That paper clip is one hundred."

Eitan turned wide eyes on Becca as the demon cackled at a pitch so high Becca was afraid it might shatter the jar the way those opera ladies shattered wineglasses in movies. She rubbed at the worry stone in her pocket, running her thumb over the polished surface to try to help her calm down and focus. Then she gasped. *My worry stone.*

"Eitan!" She sprinted back across the room to her friend's side and pressed the small purple rock into his hand.

Eitan grinned at her and held it up triumphantly, then said in a loud voice, "I'm done with this game; it's just no fun. This worry stone makes one hundred and *one*!"

The mazzik's eyes narrowed. The spot where Becca assumed its face was contorted in fury. It let out a wordless shriek and flailed its limbs like it was trying to stamp all of its footlike appendages at once.

"It's not fair!" it yelled, still writhing. "This was supposed to be an easy job! 'Just haunt the girl,'" it said in a fake deep voice like it was imitating someone. "'She won't see the magic, just the mischief. It'll be fun.'" The mazzik stamped its feet again. "Well, I'm *not. Having. Fun!*" It started shrieking again. The little creature was rapidly shifting from a muddy green to a brownish red that got brighter and brighter until it was the color of a cartoon tomato. With one last scream of fury, the mazzik exploded in a puff of sparks and smoke.

There was a cracking noise. Before Becca had a chance to react, Eitan dove at her and threw his jacket over both their heads. A split second later, the jar the mazzik had been in burst outward. Becca heard tiny shards of glass hitting the jacket like drops of rain.

Eitan didn't move for a long moment after the glass stopped falling. The only sound in the silence was their rapid breathing. Becca pushed at her friend's shoulder, and he startled a little, then seemed to realize that he was still crouching over her, holding his jacket like a shield. He straightened up, reaching out a hand to pull Becca to her feet. Both of them winced a little as fragments of glass fell from Eitan's jacket to the floor, but Becca could tell from the way her skin had stopped crawling that the danger had passed.

"Holy smokes," she said. It felt like the best way to sum up the craziness that had been the last half hour of their life.

Eitan nodded. "You said it. Here." He held out her worry stone. "Thanks for the loan. You saved the day."

Becca took the stone and put it back in her pocket. "You're the one who came up with all the rhymes," she said.

"All right," Eitan said. He was starting to grin, and Becca could feel herself smiling back. It was probably the adrenaline, she decided. There was no other reason for her to feel so giddy after what was arguably the strangest thing that had ever happened to her—and that was counting the demons with the super-stretchy arms. "A team effort, then," Eitan continued. "We both saved the day." He offered his fist with a hopeful grin, and

Becca tapped her own fist against it. "And," Eitan said, still grinning, "we even have time to go catch most of Nae's show!" They could hear the faint sounds of music from the auditorium.

"Will they let us sit in on a dress rehearsal?" she asked.

Eitan shrugged. Apparently defeating a tiny demon that called itself "a destroyer" was enough to make Eitan forget how worried he had been earlier about breaking the rules. "If anyone asks, we'll just say we're here to pick up Naomi and came early."

"All right, sure," Becca said. She looked around the room at the mess they had created. Broken glass glittered on the carpet around them, every drawer was open, and every shelf had been swept clean of its contents. Art supplies were scattered in random piles around the room, and most of the floor was covered in paper like a very colorful snowdrift. The yellow dreidel sat on top of it all, not even scratched. Becca put it in her pocket with her worry stone. She'd give it back to the twins later. "We should probably clean some of this up first, though."

Eitan spun in a slow circle, taking in the

wreckage. "You really made a mess, huh, Becks?" he said faintly.

"I was in a hurry!"

"Fair enough." Eitan sighed. "Well, maybe we'll make it by intermission."

6

A HAUNTING

"I can't believe I missed the goblin literally exploding!"

"It's not a goblin," Becca reminded Naomi for what felt like the hundredth time.

"Okay, but it basically is, and you got it to explode by *counting*? And the whole time I was just in the auditorium singing about crow's-feet." She threw herself backward on Becca's bed. It had taken them several hours split over a couple of days to put her room to rights without Becca's parents noticing, but they had done it. Becca was grateful that her bed was a cheap, low bed frame from one of the big box stores. She didn't think they would have been able to flip the frame over by themselves otherwise. Now they had the house to themselves for the first time that week. Becca's dad had gone to an interview, and her mom was taking the twins to the free after-school dance class at the community center.

Becca didn't know where Jake was, and really, she didn't care. Her brother had been getting more and more unpleasant with each passing day. He had never been a particularly nice kid, but the ugliness Becca was seeing from him now made her worry. The worry didn't make Becca any less angry at Jake, though. He was supposed to be helping Becca look after the twins, not adding to the number of people she had to look after. *I'm supposed to be a grown-up now,* Becca reminded herself. It didn't really help. She'd stopped talking about it, because it made Naomi look sad, but she was still stuck on the whole spiritual maturity thing that the rabbi had been talking about. It felt like a code she couldn't crack. Plus, it was hard to feel grown-up when Naomi was still talking about crow's-feet. "*Ugh,*" Naomi was saying. "As if everyone needs another reminder of how women aren't allowed to age."

"I think that's actually kind of the point of that story line, Nae," Eitan said mildly. "Unconditional love and all that." He was sitting on the carpet, leaning back against the bed while he read. He was reading about mazzikim, though he had informed them with a frustrated groan that the amount of accessible material on the internet was annoyingly small. Naomi kicked him gently in the head. "Ow," he said, still not looking up from his book.

"I don't need you to tell me what the play I'm in is about," Naomi said icily. "I went through a full month of pre-rehearsal analysis with Mrs. Roberts before she even let us do a real table read."

Eitan finally put his book down and looked up at her, a wide-eyed expression on his face that Becca knew meant he was about to make trouble. "Wow, and after all that you still weren't able to grasp the subtle commentary of *The Addams Family Musical.* Mrs. Roberts must be so disappointed."

Naomi sat up with an offended yelp and proceeded to beat Eitan over the head with one of Becca's stuffed animals, yelling at him about doubting her ability as an *artist.*

"Do you think there are going to be more demons?" Becca asked loudly. Her friends froze.

Naomi still held the toy in the air, and Eitan's hands were still lifted above his head in an attempt to shield himself from the onslaught. Becca took the opportunity to grab the stuffed animal and sit herself between them. She rolled her eyes at the pinched look Naomi gave her. Naomi hated to be managed, but Becca was an expert at separating fighting kids, even when those kids were her best friends and not her five-year-old siblings. Becca stared flatly back at Naomi until she scowled and lay back down. Eitan nudged Becca's knee, grinning, but Becca only turned her blank look on him until he looked away sheepishly.

"So?" Becca said. "Was this a one-time kind of situation, or do we have to prepare for more magic to start happening?"

"It's never just a one-off situation," Naomi muttered darkly.

"Okay," Eitan said, "I don't know who made *you* the expert, but I'm not sure one previous experience with magic is enough for us to confidently use words like *never*."

"What is your *problem* today, Eitan?" Naomi demanded.

"What's *yours*?" he shot back.

"Stop!" Becca said. She was starting to feel fidgety with the rising tension in the room. They were both right, though. Both of them were especially on edge that afternoon. The two of them never fought like this. That was *Becca* and Eitan. It was Naomi who kept the peace and made sure everyone got along, but here she was picking fights with Eitan and ignoring all the signs of Becca being overwhelmed. That was very wrong. If Naomi never fought with Eitan, then she *really* never ignored Becca's distress. Becca rubbed at her arms. "You're both right," she said out loud. "I don't think we can use the Golem situation as the baseline here, but I don't think it's just a one-time thing, either. I mean . . . look at you guys. Can't you feel that something's off?"

Eitan shrugged and looked away, but Naomi looked thoughtful. "I can't," she said, "but I want to try something." She hopped up off Becca's bed and headed toward the door. "Come on."

Becca scrambled to her feet. Eitan moved more slowly. "Where are we going?"

"Just come on," Naomi said impatiently. "I'm doing an experiment."

"So you're just using us as guinea pigs? Don't

you have your worms for that kind of thing?"

Naomi's expression crumpled, and Becca grimaced. Separating a physical fight was one thing, but Becca had never been very good at playing peacekeeper. Instead, she did the most straightforward thing she could think of. She grabbed Eitan's wrist and pulled. He protested loudly, but Becca didn't let go. She shoved Naomi out the door ahead of them and kept dragging Eitan behind her until Naomi had led them out the front door and across the front lawn. As soon as Becca's feet hit the sidewalk, a nearly physical weight she hadn't even really realized was there lifted off her chest and shoulders. She took a shuddering breath.

Eitan was still on the grass, leaning back to try to free his arm from her grip. "*Rebecca Reznik,* I swear to—" Becca gave another sharp tug that sent Eitan toppling forward, nearly causing him to crash into Naomi. "Becca!" Eitan yelled and then, "Oh."

Naomi wrapped her arms around him and rested her chin on his shoulder. "Yeah," she said. "That was kind of what I was afraid of." She took a deep breath and squeezed Eitan even tighter.

Eitan squeaked, but didn't try to get away from the hug.

"I'm sorry, Eitan," Naomi said.

"Me too," Eitan mumbled.

Becca sighed and shuffled a little closer until she was pressed shoulder to shoulder with Naomi as well. Naomi turned her head to smile at her and leaned in to the contact.

"So, Becca's house is haunted," Eitan said.

Naomi groaned and let go of him. "You can never just let a hug happen, huh?"

"Hey! I let hugs happen all the time! I'm a great hugger! I'm just saying. We all felt it."

Naomi nodded. "Oh, for sure. Becca's house is haunted by goblins."

"It wasn't a goblin!" Becca protested.

"I don't think it's just that one, either," Eitan added. Becca glared at him, and he shrugged. "I'm just saying. That one kind of went boom. It wouldn't still be haunting your house."

"Well, if she has Hanukkah goblins, there have to be at least eight of them."

Becca threw her hands in the air, nearly clipping the side of Eitan's head. "It's not even Hanukkah yet! And they're not goblins!"

Naomi bit down on her lip to hide a smile. "It'll be Hanukkah in, like, five days. And it was super early last year. Maybe the goblins' calendar is off."

Eitan snorted. "You think we have a better grasp on the Jewish lunar calendar than mystical Jewish creatures?"

"Maybe they have a different moon?"

"You're both terrible," Becca grouched. "Can we be serious?"

"I'm very serious!" Naomi protested. "I'm just also not the one in charge of the information!" She looked pointedly at Eitan, who rolled his eyes.

"What, am I supposed to link my brain right to the internet now? I don't have my notes! You didn't let me grab my backpack before you dragged me out of there," he said.

Becca sighed. "All right. I'll go get it, since I've been living in the house and I'm more used to the . . ." She waved her hand around vaguely.

"Bad vibes?" Naomi supplied.

"Sure."

"Are you really used to it, though?" Eitan asked. "You *have* seemed a little off lately. I thought it was just because of . . . you know . . . everything else, but maybe it's getting to you?"

Becca frowned at him. She had noticed that something about her house was weird. Of course she had. But she had blamed the tension between her parents and the secrets being kept from the younger kids. She hadn't thought there was anything weird about the immediate feeling of relief she had leaving home these days. It made sense, though, now that she was really paying attention. All the frustrated thoughts, all the anger, all the feelings of being left to fend for herself, they were made worse by the house. She looked at her friends. Naomi had stopped looking like she was going to laugh and was looking at Becca like maybe she was worried. Eitan, too, was staring at her with wide, worried eyes. Eitan's worried eyes were so effective even *she* never missed them. His long eyelashes and round face made his eyes seem enormous, like some kind of anxious sugar glider.

"*All right,*" she said. "So, what can we do? I still live here," she reminded them. "My whole family still lives here."

"Can we tell your family?" Naomi asked nervously.

Becca shook her head. "They'll think I'm having,

like, a nervous breakdown or something," she said. "And anyway, it's not like we could afford to stay anywhere right now."

"You could all stay with us," Naomi offered.

Becca shook her head again. "They won't," she said. "Let's just take care of this fast, okay? So things can stop feeling so terrible."

"Have you been feeling terrible?" Naomi asked, scooting closer to Becca.

Becca shrugged a little but didn't move away. It was nice, kind of, to have her friends worried about her, especially now that she realized what the house had been doing to her. "We'll fix it."

"You need to be able to think straight to fix it," Naomi said firmly. "You can't be in the bad vibes all the time."

"We'll treat it like radiation," Eitan said, like that meant anything at all to Becca. Eitan looked at her blank face and rolled his eyes a little. "We'll treat it like UV light on your maps," he corrected.

"Oh," Becca said. That made sense. UV light faded her maps, especially the antique ones, but it couldn't be avoided completely unless she never ever took them out to look at them. It was one of the reasons Becca kept her maps in tubes when she needed to carry them around or in big file folders when they were at home. "So, we try to stay away from the house as much as possible? How does that work?"

"Well, for right now, I'll go back in, since I'm over here the least," Eitan decided. "We'll have to make a plan for you to stay over at Nae's a whole bunch while we figure out what's going on."

Naomi shrugged. "We practically have sleepovers all winter break anyway," she said. "Shouldn't be hard."

"Yeah, yeah, rub it in," Eitan grumbled.

"Don't act like you're not over most of those nights, too," Naomi said.

Eitan only shrugged a little in response. His parents had started to be weird about Eitan sleeping over with them. They had tried to say it wasn't allowed at all anymore, but Naomi had had a field day. She had given Mr. and Mrs. Snyder an entire PowerPoint presentation about reinforcing heteronormative social norms and not assuming that all three of them were even straight or *wanted* to kiss people, and that by *that* logic she and *Becca* shouldn't be allowed to have sleepovers either because what if they were *lesbians*. But it hadn't really worked. Eitan's parents had listened politely, and then Mrs. Snyder said, "You guys are just growing up. Some things will change." Then Naomi convinced her moms to get involved and that worked a little better, so Eitan was allowed at sleepovers if it *was all three of them*, since apparently that counted as having a chaperone, or something.

It was, in Becca's opinion, completely ridiculous, but she hadn't wanted to talk to *her* parents about it and risk another *talk* like the one her mom had given her about her period. So they were left with the compromise: Eitan was only allowed over after 10:00 p.m. when it was all three of them, and the door had to be open the whole time if he was alone with either Naomi or Becca. It had made things very awkward between the three of them for a week or two, until Naomi had put her foot down and announced that just because their parents were being weird didn't mean *they* had to be. It hadn't totally worked until she had gone so far as to threaten to make Eitan kiss her to prove that there wasn't going to be any *changing* in their relationship. Eitan had scrambled backward so fast he had almost fallen off Naomi's bed, and Becca had laughed hard enough that she did fall off, and that had been that. Eitan still pouted about it, though.

"Listen," Becca said, trying to be comforting, "if I'm over at Nae's a lot, then that means you can stay over more, right?"

Eitan perked up a little at that.

"Okay, great," Naomi said. "So, Eitan is going to go in and get his stuff, and then we're all going to bail out to my house and figure out how to banish goblins."

"They're not goblins," Becca and Eitan said together. Becca narrowed her eyes at her friend—she didn't like it when she and Eitan were on the same page; as Naomi would say, it meant something was about to get real—but Eitan was already turning back to the house with a look on his face like he was solving a math problem.

"It's not on fire, Eitan," Naomi said. "You can just go in."

"I'm going!" Eitan said. He took off running. He was fast. Becca always forgot that, since Eitan mostly did chess club as his after-school activity, but he had been going running with his dad every morning since he was eight. He was out of the house and across the yard again in just a few minutes, lugging his heavy backpack behind him and bending over to catch his breath.

Becca eyed the backpack. "That's more stuff than you brought with you from home," she said.

"I got your toothbrush and pj's," Eitan panted, "and a change of clothes and a few pairs of socks, since you don't like to wear Nae's."

"They're too tight," Becca said automatically, and then what Eitan had said actually caught up to her. She blinked at her friend, feeling something itchy in her throat like she was maybe going to cry. Naomi was beaming at them.

"Thanks," Becca said softly.

Eitan grinned at her and punched her in the shoulder. "Obviously!" he said.

"Did you get her a bra?" Naomi asked.

Becca felt her whole face turn red. "Naomi!"

"What? You don't like mine either. You say they're scratchy."

Becca gaped at her. Naomi's bras *were* scratchy, and they weren't even the right size, but still.

Eitan cleared his throat. "I did, actually," he said. "I didn't go through your drawers or any-thing!" he said quickly, seeing the expression on Becca's face. "But you have talked about that too!"

Naomi smiled at Eitan happily, like she was proud of him for being so thoughtful.

Becca groaned. "Okay. Thank you for that, too."

Eitan's grin returned. "You're welcome! Now text your parents. I bet you can stay at Nae's the whole weekend if we play our cards right."

"What about the show?" Becca asked.

Naomi said a word that would have definitely meant they weren't getting a sleepover if either of her moms had heard it. "I forgot about tech week rules."

"Maybe we can get an exception?" Eitan asked. "Tell them Becca's really having a hard time?"

"I don't like lying to Nae's moms," Becca mumbled.

"It's barely a lie," Eitan reasoned.

"It's true, Becks," Naomi said. "You are having a hard time, and you really need to get out of the house." She pulled out her phone and said into the speaker, "Call Mama."

"Don't worry," she said to Becca as it rang. "The Mothership is super empathetic to teenage emotional turmoil. They'll definitely say yes."

7

PLUMBING ISSUES

It turned out Naomi was right about her moms saying yes. For all of Naomi's exaggerated pleading, all it took was a single sniffle from Becca and Miss Miriam was on her way to get them, to heck with her afternoon yoga class. Well. She hadn't said "heck," but Becca wasn't allowed to swear, so she tried not to, even in her head.

"You know we could have walked, Mama," Naomi said as she clambered into the back seat. Becca followed after her. Eitan always got the front seat, "on account of his delicate constitution," as Naomi liked to say.

"I know you could have walked," Miss Miriam

said, turning around to make sure they were all buckled in, "but you guys just sounded so sad." Her long braid—the inspiration for Becca's hairstyle of choice—hung over the side of the seat as she smiled gently at Becca. There was a piece of floaty, colorful fabric tied around the end of it. It matched the swirls of color on her workout bodysuit. She had thrown a vintage, oversize denim jacket covered in political patches and pride pins over her yoga clothes, and Becca thought she looked very stylish. Both of Naomi's moms always looked very stylish, but Becca loved Miss Miriam's style in particular. It felt like it belonged to her, instead of looking like everyone else's idea of fashionable. It made Becca feel like maybe she didn't have to try so hard to look like everyone else.

"Thanks for coming to get us," she said.

"Of course, sweetie!" Miss Miriam said. She patted Becca's knee once before turning back around and putting the car into drive. "Anything for my Becca-bean, you know that! Now, what do you want for dinner tonight?"

"Grilled cheese," Naomi said immediately.

"I don't think I was asking you, Nomes," Miss Miriam said. "Becca?"

"I like grilled cheese," Becca said.

Miss Miriam shook her head. "Of course you do." She glanced sideways. "Am I feeding you too, Eitan?"

"Yes, please, Mrs. Teitelbaum."

"Oh, honey, call me Miss Miriam. Mrs. Teitelbaum is my wife."

Naomi groaned as Eitan and Miss Miriam giggled. Becca shook her head. Miss Miriam loved to tell that joke. It was the only reason Eitan ever called her "Mrs. Teitelbaum." He thought it was funny too.

"I hate you guys," Naomi said. "I'm taking Becca and we're going to run away and live in West Hollywood with Uncle David."

Miss Miriam snorted. "You think your uncle David's jokes are any better than mine? Besides, Uncle David won't make you grilled cheese."

That seemed like a fair exchange to Becca. She was always happy to put up with Miss Miriam's silly sense of humor in exchange for her extremely consistent cooking.

Miss Miriam pulled the car through the gate in front of the Teitelbaums' house and up the driveway. "All right," she said. "Go play. I don't want to see any of you until it's dinnertime unless it's an emergency, or you need help with your homework, or you wanted to help with dinner, or you missed me, or—"

"Okay, thanks, Mama!" Naomi said, grabbing her backpack and scrambling out of the car. "We'll see you for dinner in an hour or two!"

Becca and Eitan said their own thank-yous and followed Naomi out of the car at a much slower pace. She was already sprawled across her bed when they got upstairs, flipping through a familiar picture book.

Becca scowled at her. "I told you they weren't goblins," she said.

"I'm just making sure we cover all possible areas of research," Naomi said innocently.

Eitan rolled his eyes. "Sure you are." He opened his backpack and pulled out all of Becca's stuff, shoving it into the drawer in her dresser that Naomi left empty exactly for that purpose. Then he turned around and pulled out a large book and his laptop before dumping the now-empty bag on the floor and settling in next to Naomi.

"Mazzikim," he said, giving Naomi a pointed

look, "called devils or destroyers, are invisible demons that exist everywhere. The Talmud says they're responsible for all the small annoyances we have every day, like clothes wearing out, sore feet, stubbed toes, that kind of thing."

Becca scrunched her face up at him. "That's stupid," she said. "Clothes wear out because of friction."

Eitan didn't even bother to look up. "And demons don't exist," he retorted. "Besides, I'm not the one writing it. I'm just sharing facts." He flipped to another page in the book, then sighed and turned back to his laptop. "All the sources are kind of repeats of the text, but basically there's supposed to be so many of these demons that they basically surround us, but we can't see them. Apparently that's a good thing." He turned back to the book and read, "'If the eye had the power to see them, no creature could endure the mazzikim.' Though no one seems to be able to tell me what they mean, exactly, by 'endure.'"

"Okay," Becca said slowly, "so we definitely don't want to try to make them all visible. But what can we do about them?"

"Well, first I would make sure that it is just

mazzikim," Naomi said. "Tell me again exactly what it said to you."

"It said it wasn't fair," Becca repeated dutifully for what was probably the fifth time. "It said this was supposed to be an easy job! 'Just haunt the girl,' that I wouldn't see the magic, just the mischief."

"So someone put it up to messing with your room."

"What about the rest of the house?" Eitan asked.

"It didn't turn the rest of the house upside down," Becca said.

"No, but something's doing *something*." Eitan waved his hands around. "Because of the vibes."

"The vibes are rancid," Naomi said sagely. "Rancid demon vibes."

Becca made a face at her friend. "That's not actually helpful, Nae."

"Sure it is. Eitan, search for demons that mess up vibes."

Eitan's fingers on the keyboard didn't move. "All demons mess up vibes, Nae, and no one writing serious material about them is going to use the word 'vibes' or 'rancid.'"

"You don't know," Naomi said loftily. Becca hit

her with a pillow. "Okay! Sorry! No vibes! Eitan, is there anything there about something that could control the mazzikim?"

Eitan did start typing then. "Not really," he said. "Or, yes, but it depends who you ask." He turned to show them. Becca took one look at the dozens of tabs open on his screen and tuned him out. She was missing something. She could feel it like an itch under her skin. She scratched at the back of her neck. There was a strange sound coming from somewhere down the hall.

"Guys?"

"Like the sources talk about a demon hierarchy. They have a king and everything, but none of them are clear on whether any of the demons actually listen to anyone," Eitan was saying. "They're kind of just chaotic."

"*Guys*," Becca said again. The air felt like it was suddenly full of static electricity. Becca could feel the hair on her arms beginning to stand up. There was a sound like a splash followed by the kind of gurgle made by dropping something large and empty into a pool of water—Becca could practically see the giant bubbles rushing to the surface as the thing sank. "Do you hear that?"

All the humor disappeared from Naomi's face, and she scrambled across the bed so she could peer at Becca. "What are you hearing? Are you itchy? Besides the usual itchiness, I mean. Are you *itchy*?"

"It feels so bad," Becca whispered.

Naomi's face crumpled. She fluttered her arms in the air near Becca like she really wanted to hug her but couldn't quite figure out how to do that without making things worse. Unexpectedly, it was Eitan who stood up.

"We're not going to learn anything sitting here," he said. "Let's follow the sound." He shrugged at their surprised faces. "I've found what I'm going to find on mazzikim without us going back to Rabbi Levinson, and I don't think he'll be as willing to just believe us this time around."

That was very true. Just because the rabbi was being cool about the Golem didn't mean he would necessarily ignore another one of their "school projects." A part of Becca wanted to tell him anyway. Either he would help them and it would all be over, or he would get them in trouble and she wouldn't be able to go fight off demons. She knew that was just wishful thinking, though. The house would stay terrible if they didn't do *something*.

"Becks?" Eitan was looking at her like maybe he had said her name once already.

"Sorry." She felt her cheeks heat up. "I'm paying attention."

"Oh-*kay*. So, we're going to go check it out?"

"Yeah. Yes. Let's check it out." She pushed herself to her feet, nodding at Naomi, who also scrambled up. The three of them crowded together as Eitan peered slowly around the door.

"It's empty," he whispered. There was another splashing sound, and this time all three of them jumped. Becca tried not to feel too relieved that she wasn't the only one hearing the sounds anymore. Eitan kept his voice quiet. "I think the sound is coming from the bathroom."

"Gross," Naomi whispered back.

They piled out into the hall. The noise was louder there. And grosser. A weird bubbling gurgle like someone was trying to flush something way too big down a toilet. Naomi had a handful of the back of Becca's sweatshirt and was pressed close enough that Becca could feel her slightly too quick breath moving the little hairs that had escaped from Becca's braid. Becca stepped forward slightly, but that just put her closer to Eitan, who hadn't moved. Naomi reached past Becca and took hold of Eitan's T-shirt with her other hand. They shuffled down the hall like that, Becca crushed and squirming between the two of them, until they reached the bathroom and Eitan pulled them up short.

"Should we have, like . . . a weapon or something?"

There was a long pause. "Have we ever had a weapon?" Becca asked finally.

"Okay, good point." Eitan pushed the door open and stepped inside, shuffling sideways so Becca and Naomi could file in behind him.

At first glance nothing seemed off. Then the noise started again. It was coming from the toilet. The closed lid rattled with the gurgling that from this close sounded more like a dying jet engine than anything related to plumbing. There was a low noise in Becca's ears, like something was growling.

"Is it going to explode?" Becca asked.

"If it does, we are definitely in the line of fire," Naomi pointed out. "But also, maybe if the toilet explodes, the Mothership will finally let me put in a composting toilet."

"Ew," said Becca.

"It's much more environmentally friendly!" Naomi protested.

Becca was saved from having to reply to that particular statement when the toilet let out a belching noise that shook the lid and released a smell that wasn't as gross as Becca would have expected from a backed-up toilet but certainly wasn't pleasant. She pulled her sweatshirt up over her mouth and nose. "I'm going to open it," she decided.

"*Why?*" Eitan asked, aghast.

"What else are we going to do?" Becca demanded. "Stare at it until it explodes?"

Eitan didn't have an answer to that, so Becca disentangled herself from Naomi's grip and stepped toward the toilet. It rattled again and she flinched, but nothing else happened. She kept moving forward until she could reach out and flip the lid open with the tips of her fingers. Then she leapt back. The lid clanged loudly against the tank, and for a second Becca thought it was going to slam shut again, but it stayed open. Becca could see flecks of water flying up out of the toilet bowl, but otherwise it didn't actually seem to be overflowing. She inched forward again, standing on her tiptoes to peer into the bowl. Naomi and Eitan moved with her this time.

The water in the bowl was so agitated, it almost looked like it was boiling. And it was too dark, somehow. Not the gross, sewage-brown that Becca had been dreading, but almost black, like there was something underneath the surface casting a dark shadow. They moved even closer, careful to avoid the spray of the water, and Eitan shone his phone flashlight into the toilet. There was a noise like a wail and a growl combined and a flash of what looked like gold fur under the water. Then it was silent. The toilet bowl was clear, still water over smooth porcelain once again, and Becca knew that whatever it was had gone. The demanding itch under her skin had disappeared.

"Um," Eitan said.

Naomi sighed. "No compost toilet for me, I guess. Was it another goblin, do you think?"

"There's never even been one goblin," Becca said. "But yeah, I think so."

"In the toilet?" Eitan said. He sounded like he didn't believe it, which seemed silly to Becca. It wasn't like it was the weirdest thing they had ever seen. Okay. Well. It might have been *one* of the weirdest things they had ever seen, but it definitely wasn't *much* weirder than anything else.

"You ever hear of a toilet demon?" Becca asked.

"No," Eitan said.

Naomi stuck her head forward so that she was between them. "Should we get out of the bathroom, or does one of you want to explain to my moms what we're all doing in here together?"

Becca met Eitan's startled look with one of her own. Naomi snorted at them, then whisper-shouted "hey!" as they both shoved past her to race back down the hall to Naomi's room.

"You guys are so dramatic," she scolded as she followed them at a more reasonable pace and shut the door quietly behind her.

"*You* have a weird and mature relationship with your parents, full of communication and open conversations about sex. *Our* parents have mortifying and awkward talks with us about hormones." Eitan shuddered. "I don't need to hear about how as I get older I'm going to have *urges* ever, *ever* again."

Becca patted his shoulder sympathetically. Naomi just rolled her eyes.

"Dramatic," she repeated. "*Anyway*, there's something in my toilet. What is it?"

Eitan shrugged. "I'll look into it, but . . ." He trailed off, giving Becca a look she didn't know how to interpret.

"What?" she demanded.

"It's just . . . nothing's been magical in Naomi's house until tonight."

"So?"

"So maybe it's not your house that's haunted, Becks. Maybe it's you?"

8

THE SCIENTIFIC METHOD

The solution, apparently, to Eitan declaring Becca haunted, Naomi insisting that her "vibes were flawless as usual," and Becca herself insisting that one instance of a plumbing issue didn't necessarily mean anything, was to conduct an Experiment.

"An Experiment," Eitan explained, and he did say the word as though it came with a capital letter, "needs to be able to be replicated before it can be considered valid."

"Okay?" Naomi was using her patient voice, which meant she was going to stop being patient very, very soon. "So what do we do then?"

Eitan tapped his chin. "We need to bring Becca to as many toilets as possible and see if the thing shows up."

"Absolutely not," Becca said.

"For science!" Eitan cried.

"Not on your life."

Naomi let out a long sigh. "He's right, Becks"—she sent Eitan an exasperated look—"unfortunately."

Becca stared at her friend in betrayal, but Naomi only shrugged. "Wow. Okay," Becca said. "So, which toilets do you have in mind?"

Eitan looked thoughtful. "Let's start with my house. You guys can come over for a few hours when Miss Miriam drops me off tomorrow, and we'll see if anything pops up in my bathroom. Then school, obviously."

Becca shuddered. "Why school?"

"Because it's the easiest place for us to find a bathroom outside of our houses?" Eitan was giving her a look, but Becca wasn't all that interested in trying to interpret it.

"I don't even use the school bathrooms when I have to pee!" she said. "Why would I use them to try to test if I'm haunted?"

There was a pause. "Becca," Naomi groaned, "we've talked about this."

"No, *you* talked about it," Becca said.

"Okay, I know that when we were in, like . . . sixth grade, it was scary to use the bathroom with the older kids, but we *are* the older kids now. You know you're going to give yourself an infection."

"Um—" Eitan started. The girls ignored him.

"I'm not going to get an infection," Becca scoffed, trying to ignore how close Naomi's "we are the older kids now" sounded to what Becca had been telling herself about being a grown-up. "I always go right when I get home. Right before I eat my snack."

"That is not often enough, Becks! That's, like, eight hours!"

"Guys!" Eitan was looking distinctly red-faced. "Can you have this conversation when I'm not here?"

"Why?" Naomi asked.

"Because I don't need to know about Becca's bodily functions!"

"You're not worried about her?"

"No, he's not," Becca cut in, "because it's a weird thing to be worried about!"

Naomi narrowed her eyes. "Deena got a UTI last year, and it was really bad," she said. "Maybe you should talk to my moms—"

"*Anyway*, Eitan was talking about dragging me to different bathrooms because he apparently secretly hates me, or something," Becca said.

"It's for science!" Eitan threw his hands up and stomped toward the bedroom door. "I'm going to go help Miss Miriam with dinner. We'll try my bathroom tomorrow."

The school bathroom was just as horrible as Becca had worried it would be. Eitan's toilet had done the same thing as Naomi's when Becca had spent more than half an hour in his house. The water bubbled and turned black, but nothing else happened. It just gurgled threateningly and then disappeared. Becca didn't know what it meant, but she was prepared to count that as "replicated," or whatever it was that Eitan was hoping to prove. Eitan hadn't agreed, and so the three of them were crammed into the one wheelchair-accessible single bathroom in the whole school because it was the only bathroom with a door that locked.

"At least this one's cleaner than the big ones,"

Naomi said, tugging on Becca's backpack in a way that Becca figured was meant to be comforting.

It was true, but Becca wasn't in a mood to accept small victories. "It's still horrible," she muttered.

Eitan pulled Becca away from Naomi and pushed her toward the toilet. Becca leaned back as far as she could until Eitan was staggering under her weight, but he couldn't move without dropping her. "Becca!"

"Becks," Naomi said.

Becca huffed but straightened up. "Fine. But I want it known that I hate this."

"We know," Eitan grumbled. He checked his watch. "Twenty-seven minutes left for lunch. Do you think that should be enough time?"

Becca didn't snap her teeth at him, but she really wanted to. She stared at the toilet water and waited, letting Naomi remind Eitan that they didn't *know* if it would be enough time because they didn't actually know what was happening. It was a crazy thing to think, but Becca kind of missed the Golem. At least with him they knew what to blame for the magic.

When there were eight minutes left of their

thirty-five-minute lunch break, the water in the toilet began to bubble. The now-familiar gurgling sound started up, along with the grumbling-growling that only Becca could hear. The water turned black, and the toilet seat rattled. There was a flash of gold under the water, there and gone, and then the bell rang, bright and obnoxious from the speaker in the wall, and the thing was gone. Becca stared at the clear, still water.

"So?" she asked Eitan. "Replicated enough?" She turned around to look at her friend. Eitan's eyes had gone wide again, and his forehead was scrunched up. Naomi was biting her lip. None of them had made any move to grab their bags and head to class.

"We need to go back to your house," Eitan decided. "I think that's the place it's most likely to actually appear."

"Do we want it to appear?" Naomi asked. She was moving now. She put Eitan's backpack on his shoulders, pulling his arms through the straps and pulling the tabs to make the whole thing sit higher on his shoulders. Eitan imme-diately loosened them. Naomi narrowed her eyes but left him to it and turned to pretighten

Becca's straps. She held the pack out for her to shrug into. Becca left the straps tightened and even let Naomi wrap the waist strap around her. The extra pressure around her shoulders and hips helped make her feel less like she was vibrating out of her skin.

"We need it to appear," Eitan said, clicking the lock open and peering outside to check that the hallway was clear. "Otherwise this is just going to keep happening." He gave Becca a look she couldn't quite figure out and then said to Naomi, "And then Becks will never pee."

Becca scowled at Eitan, closing her mouth tight around the urge to tell him that she *had* peed since they discovered the demon . . . just really fast, and first thing when she got into the house so nothing had time to show up. It wouldn't have mattered anyway; Naomi's mouth dropped open in horror, and she nodded quickly. "Okay, you're right. We need to take care of this. Becca's house after school, okay?"

Eitan swung the door open, apparently satisfied they weren't going to get caught. Becca followed her friends out into the hall and toward their fifth-period science class.

"Good thing you don't have a show tonight," Eitan said.

Naomi groaned. "Seriously. I'm so glad it's just Thursdays and Fridays. Though of course the first night of Hanukkah is a show night."

"Are you doing presents before or after?" Eitan asked casually. Becca felt her stomach clench a little, but she pushed the feeling down. It wasn't logical or fair to feel jealous of Eitan and Naomi. They always had more and bigger presents than she did, and it had never mattered before.

Naomi looked at Becca out of the corner of her eye. It was an expression that was new to Becca, one she had never had to learn the meaning of before. It made her stomach clench up even more. "Before," Naomi said quietly, a little like she hoped Becca might not hear her. Becca tried not to be mad. It didn't work, just like it didn't work when she tried not to be jealous. Though she knew she wasn't jealous of the presents, not really. She was jealous of how simple their Hanukkahs were, when hers was falling apart. She sped up a little, getting through the door of the classroom as fast as she could so that they would have to stop talking as they all found their seats. Eitan patted her shoulder as he passed, and her phone buzzed in her pocket. She ignored it, and three rows back she heard Naomi sigh.

After school they convinced Becca's mom to let Naomi and Eitan squeeze into the car with the rest of the Reznik kids. It wasn't very hard; Becca's mom had been even more distracted and distant since her dad's third interview hadn't worked out. They weren't even fighting anymore. They were just quiet. The dark, tense feelings in the house had gotten so bad that Becca had started waking up early and biking over to Eitan's house so she could go running with him and his dad and drive to school with them. Her mom had tried once to get her to take Jake with her, but Jake had been getting steadily worse as well. Her brother was always terrible—everyone knew that—but he had started to get mean in ways that made Becca nervous to leave the twins alone with him. Over the weekend, she had caught him methodically cutting all the hair off Ariela's Barbies with an intense focus he usually only saved for his most violent video games. He hadn't stopped when she came into the room, either, just smirked up at her and gone back to what he was doing. Later, Benji's remote control car started smoking when he tried to start it up, and her dad had pulled a large clump of half-melted doll hair out of the gears. Becca wanted to blame the house, but she wasn't sure. A less nice part of her thought that maybe this was always who Jake was going to turn into.

The house was definitely horrible, though. The suffocating tension hit as soon as they reached the driveway, and Eitan and Naomi both shuddered when they walked through the front door. Naomi looked like she might be sick.

Her mom didn't look like she noticed, but her shoulders were pulled up to her ears and she was clenching her jaw hard enough that Becca could see it. "Ants on a log for snack?" Becca's mom asked them.

Becca looked at her. She wanted to say yes. She loved ants on a log, and it was snack time. It felt normal, and she wanted things to feel normal for a little bit. Then Jake let out a screech of fury at Benji, who had tripped and accidentally knocked Jake's game out of his hand. She shook her head at her mom. "Not hungry," she said, ignoring the growling in her stomach that she was pretty sure her mom could hear. "We're going to go upstairs." She stepped sideways to get between Jake, who had curled his hands into fists, and Benji, then hoisted Benji up onto her back. "Come on, Ari," she said, waving her other little sibling over. Ariela went over without complaining and grabbed on to Benji's ankle. She kept Becca between her and Jake as much as she could. Becca pretended not to notice. "I'll get the twins set up with their shows," she told her mom and headed for her dad's office, Eitan and Naomi following behind her.

Eitan put on the educational shows the twins liked to watch after school, and Naomi fussed around the twins, making sure they had blankets and granola bars. Then Becca patted them both on the head twice, smiling back at them when they grinned up at her.

"Mom's going to head out for her nighttime class soon, but we're just going to be down the hall, okay, munchkins?" she said. "Stay here, and don't bug Jake. Shout if you need something."

Benji gave her a thumbs-up and Ariela waved a lazy hand without looking away from the screen. Becca figured that meant they got it.

"Come on," she said, and led her friends out,

making sure to shut the door tightly behind them. "Let's stay in my room until my mom leaves, and then we can figure it out."

"Um," Eitan said, "I'm not sure that's going to work out."

"What? Why?" Then Becca heard it. The gurgling sound that had been following her for days. It was louder now, and she could hear the toilet rattling from down the hall. She sprinted to the bathroom, nearly tripping from how loud the growling in her ears was now. The toilet water was roiling, black, and greasy, and the gold they kept seeing was flickering in and out of sight too quickly for her to track. Then something new happened: a scrabbling noise like something was climbing the pipes. The water disappeared completely, leaving only shadows, and something moving inside them.

A huge paw appeared and latched on to the side of the toilet bowl. Another followed, scraping against the porcelain as the thing in the toilet pulled itself upward. Becca had seen pictures of mountain lions with smaller, less intimidating claws. She stepped back, stumbling into Naomi, who hissed in a breath when Becca trod on her foot. There was a great sucking noise, and then a face appeared over the edge of the toilet bowl. The creature's head was huge and heavy, golden and furred like a lion but with curving tusks curling up from its lower jaw and wide, bulbous, multi-colored eyes that reminded Becca of the class goldfish. It was impossible for something that large to have come up through the pipes, but here it was, shaking water off its mottled gold fur and drooling on the bathroom tile. There was another, smaller gurgle, and a tail snaked its way over the creature's head. The tail was green and covered in thick scales. Behind Becca, Eitan muttered something about alligators in the sewers.

"Well," Naomi said faintly. "The haunting is definitely *stronger* in the house."

9

(NOT) ANOTHER GOBLIN

There was a long, frozen moment. Then Becca said, "Nope." She pushed her friends out of the bathroom and slammed the door shut. Then she thought of something, opened it just wide enough to fit her hand through, and clicked the lock button. She shut the door again and pulled the key off the top of the door.

"Do you think that's going to hold it?" Eitan asked.

"It doesn't have opposable thumbs," Becca said. "It can't open the door. The lock is so the munchkins don't go in."

"Where are we going?" Eitan asked at the same time Naomi said, "Don't you think it can break through the door?"

"Outside to think. Come on. And the mazzik couldn't." Becca remembered being confused by the tiny creature not being able to open the door, but she was ready to believe it was just some kind of strange magic rule. She could work with rules.

"Is that a mazzik?" Naomi asked doubtfully as they snuck down the stairs and out the kitchen door. "It doesn't look like the other one. It's pretty . . . big." Her face lit up. "Maybe this one is really a goblin! Quick! Eitan! Pull up the book!"

"It's not a goblin!" Becca said, but Eitan had already opened the book on his phone. He held it up once they reached the sidewalk so they could both see.

"The second goblin *is* a lot bigger," he said.

"Ooooh, that's the one that wants the pickles!" Naomi bounced on her toes and tapped so the book went to the next page and the picture of the fat, spiny goblin with its hand stuck in the pickle jar appeared. "Do you have pickles in the house, Becks?"

"It's not Hanukkah until Thursday, and I don't

have Hanukkah goblins," Becca repeated. "Eitan, see if there's anything online about demons that come out of toilets."

"There is one," Eitan said. He sounded a little frustrated. "I told you I found it yesterday."

Becca looked at Naomi, who shrugged. "Tell us again?"

Eitan rolled his eyes but pulled out his notebook. "The demon who haunts the bathroom is called bar Shirika Panda. It's . . . There's not really a description, but—" He cleared his throat and read, "It says, 'On the head of a lion and on the nose of a lioness we found the demon named bar Shirika Panda. With a bed of leeks I felled him, and with the jaw of the donkey I struck him.'"

"The jaw of a *donkey*?" Naomi shook her head. "Sorry, Becks, you just have a haunted bathroom now. We'll get you lots of cranberry juice so you don't get an infection."

Becca groaned. "What if we had, like, replacements? Like how you swap things out in a recipe."

Eitan pulled a scrunched-up face. "Like what?"

Becca stared at him, her mind blank. She wasn't even sure what leeks were.

"Let's go in and see what we have!" Naomi said.

What they had, it turned out, was a small bag of sad, tiny onions that Eitan said were shallots and that the internet said were a good substitute for leeks in a recipe and a Beanie Baby.

"It's not even a donkey," Becca said skeptically, looking at the floppy, plastic-pellet filled horse. It was cute. There was a white diamond on its forehead. It was definitely not the jaw of a donkey.

"Well, it's not like you had bits of donkey in the fridge, Becks," Eitan said. "We do what we can." He tossed the bag of shallots from hand to hand. "What's the plan here?"

Becca shrugged, snatching the shallots from the air the next time Eitan let go of it and giving the bag an experimental toss of her own. "I bet I could throw these hard enough that it would count as being 'felled,'" she said. "And then we just have to . . . hit it with the horse."

Naomi snorted. "Whose job is that?"

"Nose goes!" Eitan shouted, nearly poking himself in the eye with how quickly he jabbed his finger at his own nose.

Naomi groaned but didn't even try to touch her nose. "Fine. I will risk my life and hit the weird lion alligator toilet monster with a Beanie Baby."

That made Eitan pause. Becca wasn't completely sure what the expression he was making meant, but it seemed like he was maybe upset about something. Or uncomfortable. "I'll do it," he said.

"What?"

"I'll hit the thing with the horse, Nae. You shouldn't put yourself in danger."

Becca had no trouble at all understanding Naomi's expression. It was her *Eitan has gone absolutely crazy and needs sense talked into him* expression. She had worn it a lot since they got to eighth grade. "What are you talking about?" Naomi asked. "You won nose goes fair and square."

"But I shouldn't let you—"

"*Eitan Snyder*," Naomi said, sounding very much like her mom when she was yelling at someone on the phone. "You better not be about to say what I think you're about to say." She pinched the bridge of her nose—another move she had picked up from her mom—and muttered, "I'm going to have to make another PowerPoint presentation."

"No more PowerPoints!" Eitan said. "I'm just saying that I should be—"

"Tell me why!" Naomi said, pointing her finger in Eitan's face. "Tell me why, right now, and if it's any reason besides outdated, patriarchal—"

"Okay!" Eitan swatted at Naomi's hand. "Stop pointing at me. I'll let you hit the monster with the Beanie Baby! Yeesh!"

"Fine," Naomi said, sounding pleased. "All right."

Becca rolled her eyes. "Can we do this, please? Before that thing eats one of my siblings?"

"It might not be so bad if it ate Jake," Naomi pointed out.

"Naomi!"

"Fine! Yes, okay, let's go do this thing."

They crept back up the stairs, careful not to let Jake or the twins hear them moving around. Becca could feel the crawly itchiness of magic building on her skin, though she had been so covered in it for the last few days she barely noticed the difference. There were soft thumping noises coming from the bathroom, not as loud as Becca would have expected from a creature that size but definitely noticeable. She pushed the key into the lock, trying to unlock it as quietly as possible. She felt Naomi flinch at the click, but the demon on the other side didn't make any noise besides the soft thumping they could still hear. Becca eased the door open.

The demon was lying in the corner of the bathroom behind the toilet—Becca had no idea how it had managed to wedge its huge body back there. It was on its stomach like a cat, its chin resting on its folded paws. The thumping noise was its tail flicking gently back and forth and hitting the wall on every other twitch. It blinked slowly at them as they entered, and then a low growl began to build from deep in its chest. The sound expanded outward until Becca could feel it like a physical thing, vibrating at the base of her head and making her vision go blurry. Becca didn't get the feeling that this demon could talk, but she could feel the way it was sizing them up, lazy and unhurried. It clearly didn't think they were a threat. The horrible vibes that had been flooding her house were worse near the demon, too. The inky black liquid that had been in the toilet was sort of . . . pooling around it in the air, but it wasn't spreading out like a real liquid would.

Becca stepped fully into the bathroom. She felt Eitan and Naomi follow her and heard one of them close the door behind them. The demon's growling got louder, and Becca clenched her teeth against the onslaught. Then it stood up, and it was so much bigger than she expected. It seemed to unfold itself from the space under the toilet and then just . . . keep going. She gulped as the monster stalked toward them, the dark liquid moving with it. It was spreading now. It filled the spaces behind the demon, seeping into the corners of the room until only the area directly around Becca and her friends still held any light at all, and that was beginning to go gray at the edges. Becca's head felt like it was splitting open under the combined pressure of the real growls coming from the creature and the growling in her ears that just seemed to be one of the more terrible signs of magic getting too close to them. She was itchy everywhere. It made it impossible to concentrate.

"Do it," Eitan whispered. "Becca. Do it. Hit it. Fell it with the shallots."

Becca scrambled with the bag of tiny onions, searching for the opening in the plastic mesh. Finally, she gave up and tore at it, ripping a hole large enough to fit her hand through. Her fingers closed around the small, hard shape of the vegetable, and she felt more than saw Eitan and

Naomi scramble backward to give her room as she wound up to throw. The shallot hit the demon squarely on the nose. It stopped its advance, blinking in confusion and trying to look cross-eyed at its own snout. Then the demon shook itself, and the growling started again, even louder than before.

"Again!" Eitan said urgently. "Hit it again!"

Becca hit it with a second shallot and then a third; each time it slowed the demon down for a shorter and shorter period, until the fourth one bounced harmlessly off its head and rolled to a stop in front of Eitan.

"Naomi?" Becca whispered.

Naomi lurched forward with a shout like she was She-Ra or something and brought the Beanie Baby down hard on the demon's back. The demon stumbled, mewling a little, then turned on Naomi with a snarl. Naomi hit the thing again, and it swung a huge paw at her, knocking her backward into Becca. Eitan caught them both when Becca staggered, then kept moving with the momentum, pulling them both out the door and back into the hall, where they collapsed in a heap. Eitan was up again almost immediately, scrambling toward them and taking Naomi from Becca so he could make her lie down on the floor of the hall and pat his hands over her face and stomach while she swatted at him and tried to get up.

"Stay *still*," he said. His voice was choked and raspy, like he was trying hard not to cry.

"I'm fine," Naomi said. She tried to push herself up to sitting and winced. "Well, maybe I'll stay here for just a second," she amended, "get my breath back."

"Lift up her shirt, Becca," Eitan instructed. "We need to make sure the claws didn't get her."

"There's no blood," Becca pointed out, but after a quick look at Naomi to make sure it was okay, she did as she was told and rolled Naomi's shirt up over her rib cage. Becca and Eitan both hissed in a breath at the ugly purple bruise that was already forming along Naomi's right side. Thankfully, there didn't seem to be any claw marks.

Eitan prodded at the skin gently. "Did it get any ribs, Nae? Any trouble breathing?"

Naomi took a deep breath. It didn't look comfortable, but she could do it, which Becca thought was good news. "No broken ribs," Naomi reported. "Mostly just knocked the wind out of me, I think.

And of course . . ." She gestured at the spreading bruise.

"Could there be internal bleeding?" Becca asked.

Eitan pulled out his phone, then nearly fumbled it when a crash against the bathroom door made them all jump. He looked from the door to Becca nervously, and Becca tapped the phone screen. "One thing at a time," she said. "Internal bleeding?"

Eitan nodded and went back to his search. "Okay," he said. "This says that the signs of internal bleeding are a hard or tender abdomen—"

"Check," Naomi said.

"Bruised isn't the same as tender, necessarily," Becca pointed out, "and the skin doesn't feel hard."

Naomi shrugged. She didn't seem nervous, but Becca was pretty sure that was on purpose. Naomi could be very good at faking feelings when she needed to. As she was always reminding them: she was an *actress*. "What else, Eitan?" Naomi asked.

"Um, extensive bruising." His eyes flickered nervously to the side. "Tenderness in the chest, severe pain when you press on the stomach—"

Becca poked Naomi in the stomach.

"Hey!"

"Would you call that severe?" Becca asked.

"I'd call it rude!" Naomi exclaimed. "But no, I guess not. Definitely just sore."

"Okay," Eitan said. "Also nausea or vomiting"—Naomi shook her head—"or bleeding from the . . . um . . . the rectum or . . . uh . . . the . . ."

"Vagina," Naomi supplied helpfully.

"Yeah, that," Eitan said. "Or bloody pee."

"Ew."

"Yeah."

"Well, we don't know if I have any of the last one," Naomi said, "but I'm not nauseated and my ribs feel okay, and it was okay when Becca poked me." She pulled her shirt down over her stomach and managed to sit up for real, without leaning on Becca. "I'm going to go ahead and say I'm not bleeding internally, but I'll let you guys know if I start to feel worse." She made a face. "The show on Thursday's going to *suck*, though."

The door shook again. The demon was snarling, and it sounded like it was swiping at the door with its claws.

"What do we do about that?" Naomi asked.

They looked at Eitan, who shrugged. "That's all

the information I have," he said. "Maybe we need a real donkey jaw?"

"It's not going to happen," Becca said. "There has to be something else. Read it again."

Eitan pulled his notebook out and flipped back to the right page. "'To be saved from the demon of the bathroom, let him recite as follows: On the head of a lion and on the nose of a lioness we found the demon named bar Shirika Panda. With a bed of leeks I felled him, and with the jaw of the donkey I struck him.'"

"Leeks and donkey jaws," Becca muttered, "it says right there. It must be literal. We just don't have the right stuff." She rubbed at her forehead with the heels of her palms. It felt like a riddle, and she hated those. She wasn't good at the twisty thinking. Wait. "It's literal," she repeated.

"Right," Eitan agreed. "But we don't have the things."

"No," Becca said, "I mean the instructions are literally exactly what they say. You didn't read us the first part before!" she said accusingly to Eitan.

"What are you talking about?"

"I'm talking about what we have to do. The instructions don't say 'Fell it with leeks and strike

it with the jawbone of a donkey.' Let me see that."
She took Eitan's notebook from him and stood up.
"Stay out here with Nae," she told him. "I want to
try something."

"Becca!"

Becca opened the door and pushed her way
inside before Eitan could say anything else. The
demon had retreated slightly. It was pacing back
and forth in front of the toilet now, like it was
guarding it or something. Becca took a breath, then
lifted the notebook and read out clearly. "On the
head of a lion and on the nose of a lioness we found
the demon named bar Shirika Panda. With a bed of
leeks I felled him, and with the jaw of the donkey I
struck him." The demon shuddered and grumbled
and seemed to shrink a little. Becca repeated the
words, then again, and watched as the demon
shrank down to the size of a small house cat. It
hissed and spit and tried to climb back into the toilet, but Becca lifted up the notebook one more time
and read the words as fast as she could.

"On the head of a lion and on the nose of a lioness we found the demon named bar Shirika Panda.
With a bed of leeks I felled him, and with the jaw of
the donkey I struck him!" The demon yowled and

then dissolved into a ball of black sludge. Becca watched as it slid down the toilet. It gurgled for a moment, and then the water settled and the growling in Becca's mind quieted down.

"Oh my God," Eitan said from behind her. He was standing in the now-open door, Naomi leaning heavily against him. "How did you know that would work? Also, I'm so mad at you." He gestured between him and Naomi. "We're both so mad at you. You're never allowed to bail like that again."

"The page literally said, 'To be saved from the demon of the bathroom, let him recite as follows,'" Becca said. "It's not about the stuff; it's about saying it." She held out Eitan's notebook toward him, ignoring the second part about him being mad. He didn't seem mad, and she had practiced a lot to make sure she noticed when her friends were upset with her.

"Good going, Becks," Naomi said. She peered around the bathroom. "Not too much damage, either. We can just blame the scratches on the door on Jake."

Becca bit her lip, but honestly it didn't seem like the worst plan. Jake was grounded for three weeks anyway after the doll hair incident; scratching up the bathroom seemed like something he would do. "So, what now?" she asked. The growling in her head was quiet, but the house was still making her skin crawl.

Naomi grimaced. "We'll need to figure out what's actually going on with the house," she said, "but right now I think I need a snack and an ice pack."

"Yeah," Becca agreed, trailing behind her friends as Eitan took that as his cue to move and started helping Naomi toward the stairs. "Let's do that."

10

FIRST NIGHT OF HANUKKAH

"I'm grounded," Becca said miserably, squinting at the phone in the darkness. She was curled up near the foot of her bed and had pulled the covers over her head. Her parents had not believed the story that Jake had made the scratches in the bathroom door. Mostly because her mom had decided at the last minute to drop Jake off at the local community center to play basketball on her way to work, and Becca hadn't realized. "They think I'm having, like, a mental breakdown or something. That I'm acting out because of the stress."

"Grounded for how long?" Eitan asked.

"For two weeks, starting yesterday."

"But it's been three days!" Eitan exclaimed.

Becca sighed. "I tried that on Dad, but he says yesterday was the first full day. 'The crime was committed on Monday, so it doesn't count toward the punishment,'" she quoted.

"At least they didn't take your phone," Eitan said, spinning in his desk chair. He wasn't in bed, because it was actually 4:00 p.m. on a Wednesday.

"Dad said that cutting me off from my friends completely would make whatever breakdown I'm having worse, supposedly. But I'm not allowed to sleep over for the weekend anymore."

"You can't sleep over?" Eitan asked. "But you need to get out of the house! Winter break starts Friday. You'll be home all day!"

He was right. After she had spent so much of her time away lately, it was awful being back in the house for longer than just dinner and sleeping. Becca could barely wear clothes because of how raw her skin felt all the time. She could really only stand her oldest, softest tank top and pajama shorts. Even her super-soft bedsheets felt scratchy and painful on her bare shoulders. "I don't know how we're going to manage that." Becca sniffled.

She felt dangerously close to crying. "I'm sorry," she said. "I know if I can't do sleepovers, you can't either."

Eitan made a frustrated noise. "That's not even close to our biggest problem right now, Becks! Your house is possessed! I can tell through the phone that you're already spiraling."

"I'm not spiraling."

"You're spiraling a little, and Nae would agree with me if she weren't off getting ready for her play, though I have no idea how she's going to manage to sing in that tight black dress with her stomach and side bruised all over like that. At least her parents believed that she fell off her bike."

"We should have told them Jake kicked her," Becca muttered. "Then he'd be grounded too."

"First of all, who are you and when did you replace Becca with a clone so okay with lying? Second of all, you want to be stuck in the house *with* Jake?"

"Fair point."

"So, what's the plan?"

Becca let out a long breath. She didn't want to have to say that she didn't really have one. She felt slow and sad, and mostly she just wanted to stay there at the bottom of her bed, where the heavy covers felt a little like a safe island in the middle of a horrible ocean of terrible things. Or something. Naomi was better with words than she was. "I don't have a plan," she said finally.

Eitan made a sympathetic noise. "Hard to plan around grounded," he agreed. "We'll brainstorm. Maybe Naomi will have some thoughts. She's always better at convincing parents, anyway."

"Only because she's so annoying," Becca said.

Eitan laughed. "Okay, but at least she usually uses her powers for good. Like making sure we get to keep having sleepovers."

"That's true. Or like making sure I get to go to the show tomorrow."

"You still get to go?"

"Yeah. Naomi cried. Something about needing her best friends for support."

Eitan whooped. "And that worked? That's amazing, Becks. Should I tell my dad we need to get you?"

Becca sighed. "No. Mom says there and back only, no hanging out, and they have to drive me."

"Gross. Okay, well, it's better than nothing. At

least we can talk before the show and during intermission."

"True."

"We'll come up with something, Becks, I swear it."

Becca curled a little tighter into a ball and tried
to blink her tears away. "Okay," she whispered.

Eitan was waiting for Becca in their usual spot in
front of the school when her dad dropped her off.
That was good. It felt like a tiny piece of normal in
the middle of all the craziness. Eitan grinned when
he saw her and hopped off the wall, punching her
lightly in the shoulder.

"Feel better?"

"Yes," Becca said truthfully. She had felt better
as soon as the car had pulled out of the driveway.
She still couldn't believe that her parents couldn't
feel it. "Is your dad not staying for the show?" *Her*
dad wasn't, but that was only because he had
another phone interview that evening. Usually, all
their parents came to Naomi's shows.

"He is," Eitan said. "He already found Naomi's
moms. I told him we were going to sit somewhere
else."

"And he was okay with that?" Eitan's dad was

very into father-son bonding time. It could be very hard to convince him to leave them to their own devices.

Eitan went a little pink and shuffled his feet. "I told him I wanted to sit with you by myself." He still wasn't looking at Becca. Becca didn't mind; she thought it was strange that everyone insisted on staring at each other when they talked, but it was weird for Eitan. He was big on eye contact. "He thinks I have a crush on you," Eitan muttered.

He said it so quietly that it took Becca a second to figure out what it was he had actually said, then, "Gross."

"I know!" Eitan threw his hands up. "But they're so convinced that I'm going to end up dating one of you, I figure it's a convenient excuse."

"That's going to make sleepovers harder," Becca pointed out.

"No, it won't," Eitan said. His face was a very dark red, but he was looking at her again. "You know that's what they were worried about in the first place."

Becca shrugged. "Whatever, then. Come on." She led the way around the school to the auditorium entrance so they could get in line with their tickets. "Have you thought of anything to get me ungrounded?"

Eitan sighed. "No. But maybe we could make an argument for the weekend since it is Hanukkah? Maybe your parents will feel like taking it easy on you?"

Becca thought about it. "Maybe," she said slowly. "I think they do feel bad about Hanukkah, and they're saying I'm acting out for more positive attention, or something, so we might be able to convince them."

"You'd have to make sure they think you're really sorry and really sad."

"I am really sad," Becca said, before she could stop herself.

Eitan stopped walking. "You are?"

Becca shrugged, uncomfortable. "It's the house, mostly, I think," she said. "But also, not just the house?"

Eitan's eyes were wide. "You didn't say anything!" he said.

Becca shrugged again. "We had a lot going on."

"Okay, but we tell each other when things aren't okay. That's, like, the biggest friendship rule."

"We're supposed to be grown-up now," Becca said. "I'm not supposed to be sad."

Eitan gaped at her. "Grown-ups are sad all the time!" he shouted. Becca shushed him. "What do you mean you can't be sad because we're supposed to be grown-up? Have you never met Naomi's mama? She cries all the time!"

"That's because she thinks it's cleansing."

"Becca."

"Okay, but what about all that 'spiritual maturity' stuff we were talking about with the rabbi?"

"That's, like, the opposite of what he meant! He was talking about being able to be, I don't know, flexible with the way we think about stuff, not pretending we don't have emotions!"

"I can't really do that either!" Becca said, though she wasn't sure when this had become a fight.

"Well, we can work on it together!" Eitan was very red again, but this time Becca knew it was because he was upset.

"I'm sorry," she tried.

Eitan sighed. "You don't have to be sorry, Becks. You just have to let us be your friends. We want to help!"

"You do help."

Eitan sighed again. He scrubbed his hand over his close-cropped hair and then looked back at Becca. "Can we hug?"

Becca thought about it. She didn't love to hug, but she knew that it was how Eitan got past tough moments. Plus, she could trust Eitan to let go when she said. Becca shuffled closer and leaned forward until she could rest her forehead on his shoulder. "Five seconds," she said.

Eitan laughed a little, but he wrapped his arms around her tightly and counted to five out loud, then stepped back. He looked better. Becca was glad. "We'll figure it out, Becks," Eitan said. "They can't keep you grounded. It's the first night of Hanukkah!"

It turned out Eitan was right, though probably not in the way he had meant it. After the show—which Becca thought was a little depressing, but in which Naomi did an excellent job—Becca's dad was waiting with the car. She climbed into the passenger seat, and her dad offered her a small smile.

"Did you have a good time?" he asked.

"Naomi was glad we were there."

"How'd she do?"

"She's Nae," Becca said, which wasn't really an answer except it sort of was. Mostly Becca just didn't feel like talking to her father. He nodded and didn't say anything else until they had made it out of the school parking lot. Then he sighed a little through his nose.

"I know this is hard on you, Becca. It's been a tough couple of weeks for everyone, and you've had to take on a lot."

Becca stayed quiet. She didn't really have anything to add. Her dad was just stating facts.

"Can you tell me what really happened with the bathroom door?"

"It was an accident," Becca said. It wasn't a very convincing lie, but she wasn't particularly good at lying convincingly, and she was pretty sure her dad wouldn't believe the truth.

"How do five deep scratches end up in the bathroom door by accident? What did you even use?" Becca just shrugged, and her dad sighed again. She wished people would stop sighing at her. "I don't want to keep you grounded for Hanukkah," her dad said.

"So don't."

"Can you tell me the truth?"

Becca pressed her lips together. Her dad shook his head but didn't say anything else.

They got home just as her mom was setting up the Hanukkah candles. Ariela and Benji were with her, their small faces scrunched up in concentration as they put the candles into their own menorahs. The twins' menorahs were lumpy, misshapen blocks of clay that they had made at Hebrew school and decorated with an assortment of small plastic toys and rhinestones, but each menorah had nine little holes in a row that were the right size for candles, with one on a slightly raised ball of clay for the shamash, and the twins were very proud of them. Becca and Jake had grown out of their handmade menorahs and used smaller versions of their parents' ornate silver menorah. *That* one was a wedding present from Becca's grandparents, and none of the kids except for Becca was allowed to touch it.

Her parents made eye contact when Becca and her dad came into the kitchen, and Becca saw her mom look at her for a moment before looking back at her dad. He shook his head, and her mom sighed. Becca ignored them and went over to the table, pulling out two candles from the box to get her own menorah ready. Jake, she noticed, was nowhere to be seen. Her dad seemed to have noticed that too.

"Where's Jakey?" he asked.

Becca's mom pursed her lips. "Jacob is taking a moment to think about his actions."

Becca tried not to roll her eyes. Jake didn't "think about his actions." Most likely he was in his room with the old Nintendo DS he had swapped his friend Michael one of Becca's softball bats for. Her parents didn't know about the DS. Jake had told them that he threw away the softball bat. He had been grounded, but he kept the DS and used it when their parents took away his Switch and the controllers for his other consoles.

"What happened?" Becca's dad asked.

Becca's mom nodded her head toward the twins, who, Becca realized suddenly, had dried tear tracks on their faces.

"We're still working on respecting other people's belongings," Becca's mom said. Becca did roll her eyes then, because Jake never respected other people's belongings, but he must have done something really bad if he wasn't allowed to set up candles with them. Becca could tell her dad was thinking the same thing, because he frowned heavily and left the room. He probably wanted to *talk* to Jake about his behavior. Becca wished him luck.

Whatever conversation they had didn't take long. Becca had just finished setting up Jake's menorah for him when the brother in question stomped into the room behind their dad, looking mutinous. He shoved his way between Becca and Ariela to reach the table, and Ariela huddled back against Benji, her eyes wide.

"Move," Becca told her brother. "Switch with me."

"No," Jake growled.

She prodded at him, and he snapped his teeth at her. There was something furious in his eyes that almost made Becca step back, but Ariela's little gasp made her straighten up.

"Switch," she said. "Now."

Jake stared at her for a long moment with that horrible look. Then he blinked, and his eyes seemed to go back to normal. He scowled at her but stomped around to her other side. Becca let out a breath, and she rearranged the menorahs so they all had the right one. It made the line of menorahs look odd; they were always arranged biggest to smallest, and the family stood in that order as well. It was a change Becca didn't particularly want to make, in a Hanukkah that was already different from other years, but the twins relaxed as soon as Jake was safely on the other side of Becca. She patted Ariela's head a few times, and her baby sister smiled up at her.

"He tried to break Benji's menorah," Ariela whispered. "Mommy had to glue the shamash bit back on."

Becca was shocked. Doll hair and toy cars was one thing—one horrible, disturbing thing—but breaking the menorah was a whole other level of misbehavior. She looked over at Jake, who looked angry but definitely not sorry.

"He won't do it again," Becca promised her sister, though she didn't really believe it.

Then they had to be quiet while her mom sang the prayers and her dad helped the younger kids light their candles. Then they did presents. Becca tried to smile at her parents over the ten-dollar frozen yogurt gift certificate she unwrapped along with her customary first night of Hanukkah pair of socks. Jake was less gracious about his fifteen-dollar certificate for the comic book store. The twins were happy with their presents, at least. Ariela guarded her new doll and its long black hair from Jake with a glare that would have made Becca proud under other circumstances, and Benji took his new remote control car into the garage with their dad right away. It was an okay night, overall, even if the usual feeling of joy and celebration seemed to be missing.

Becca was helping Ariela comb her doll's hair while Ariela told her the history of the doll's lost kingdom and journey through the underworld—Ariela's stories didn't always make sense, but Becca was impressed with the creativity—when it happened. There was a loud crash from the kitchen, followed by running feet and a scream from her mother. Then her dad was charging through the room with the mini fire extinguisher. Benji followed after, clutching the remote for his car to his chest, and squatted next to Becca and Ariela.

"Jake knocked over the menorah table," he whispered.

Becca inhaled in shock just as the yelling started in the other room. Jake screamed back at her parents with a wordless shriek of rage. There was a long silence, and then her dad came into the room, rubbing his face.

"Becca, walk the twins over to the Weinsteins', please. They're going to spend the night. Can you pack their bags?"

Becca nodded.

"Thank you. Afterward you can go over to Naomi's for the weekend."

"But—" Becca started.

"You're ungrounded," her dad said. "Don't worry about it; just stay the weekend." He glanced back at the kitchen, where other crashes signaled that Jake wasn't quite done throwing things. "We'll talk when you get home." He went back to the kitchen, and Becca hurried the twins upstairs to pack their bags. She dropped them off at the Weinsteins' house—Laylah Weinstein went to the same kindergarten as the twins—then she ran home to grab her bike.

She called Naomi on her way. "I'm coming over."

"I heard," Naomi said. "Are you okay? Do you need us to pick you up?"

"No. I'm already on my bike," Becca said. "I'm okay. We need Eitan, though. Something's wrong with Jake."

11

JAKE CLIMBS
THE HOUSE

"We need to monitor him."

"How?" Eitan pulled Becca's uneaten waffles toward him. They had been having this conversation in some form or another since Becca had arrived at Naomi's the night before. Eitan had shown up not long after, and Becca had told them the whole story, but as much as they had been brainstorming, they kept getting stuck on what, exactly, they could do.

Naomi smacked Eitan's hand before he could reply and pushed the plate back in front of Becca. "Eat your lunch," she said. "We can't exactly go to your house, Becks, and Jake's not going to be allowed out."

"I have to go home eventually," Becca pointed out. She ripped off a piece of waffle and rolled it into a ball between her hands.

"Ew," Naomi said. "What's with you and balls of food?"

Becca shrugged, popping the blob of waffle into her mouth. It was good. Miss Miriam had a great recipe that tasted almost exactly like McDonald's pancakes and firmly believed in breakfast food for any meal of the day. "I like the shape. What if we went over without telling them?"

Eitan snorted. "You don't think they'll notice three extra kids in the house?"

"What if we went over to pick up the twins?" Naomi suggested.

"It could work, but they're at the Weinstein's, and anyway then we'd have the twins," Becca reminded her, "and I really don't think we want to take them with us to fight demons."

"Which brings us back to my first question, which nobody has answered," Eitan said. He took a piece of turkey bacon off Naomi's plate and pointed it at Becca. "Do you actually think your brother has been replaced by a demon?"

Becca wrinkled her nose and swatted at the bacon. "I don't know, but something's *wrong*. He's always been awful, but this is beyond that! Jake bites the dentist and picks fights with the twins. He doesn't destroy things and try to burn the house down."

"Could it just be the house?" Naomi asked. "Like the bad vibes are getting to him?"

That was something Becca had considered, but, "I don't think the house would make you do something you would really never do. It just makes you"— she cast about for the word to describe it—"thinner? Not like skinny, but like . . . worn through?"

"Raw," Naomi said.

"Yes."

"Okay, and we don't think this is just Jake's very raw self?" Eitan asked.

"He's not this bad," Becca insisted. It felt weird to be defending Jake's behavior when she had had the same thoughts about him, but she was sure now that this wasn't just her brother being his usual annoying self. "He's not . . ."

"He's not scary," Naomi finished for her. "Yeah, Becks, I see what you mean."

"So, a demon?" Eitan asked.

"Maybe," Becca said. "Do demons even replace people like that?"

"There are a few stories where that happens," Eitan said, "but it's usually someone important, like King Solomon. And they can tell by the feet."

"The feet," Becca echoed.

"Yeah, like demons can't pretend to have human feet, for some reason."

"What do their feet look like?" Naomi asked.

"I'm not sure." Eitan ate another piece of Becca's turkey bacon. "Sometimes it's chicken feet," Eitan said around his food, "but sometimes it's goat feet. Like hooves."

"Have you seen Jake's feet lately?" Naomi asked.

Becca tried to remember if she had seen her brother barefoot in the last few days. She was sure she must have, but she couldn't think of a moment. They wore socks a lot in the winter, and it wasn't like she hung out with Jake very much.

"I don't know," she admitted.

Naomi stood up. She grabbed her empty plate and Eitan's and Becca's still mostly full one, despite Eitan trying to grab it back, and took them over to the sink. She was obviously thinking, and Becca didn't even try to talk to her friend over the sound of the garbage disposal. Finally, Naomi put the rinsed plates and forks into the dishwasher and came back to the table.

"Okay, so we can get Jake alone long enough to look at his feet," she said. "We'll bike over there right now, and if your parents ask, we'll say you forgot something."

"Your socks!" Eitan volunteered.

"Sure," Naomi said. "So, we'll go over, say we're picking up some of Becca's socks on the way to the park, and see if Jake's got hooves or chicken claws."

"What if *he's* wearing socks?" Becca asked.

Her friends fell silent for a minute, thinking. Eitan opened his mouth to say something else when Miss Miriam's phone on the kitchen island started ringing loudly. The three of them startled, then shared an exasperated look about grown-ups and their loud phones.

Miss Miriam ran into the room. She was almost dressed for her 2:00 p.m. yoga class. Today's outfit was a shiny navy blue set of leggings with a matching workout top. Her hair was still down, but Becca could see the matching scrunchie around her wrist, like she had been about to put it into the braid.

"Hello?" Miss Miriam tucked the phone between her ear and shoulder and turned to smile at the three of them, but her face went serious and she turned back around, straightening up so she could hold the phone in her hand. "What? When?"

She glanced at Becca. "Of course, Sarah. We're always happy to have Becca. She can stay as long as she wants. Of course. Sure. No, I understand. Absolutely. Take care of Jake. Let us know if you need anything. All right."

Miss Miriam hung up the phone and faced them. She forced a smile, but even Becca could tell right away that it was fake. "Well, it looks like our Becca-bean is going to be staying with us for a few more days. That's fun! Maybe Eitan can stay too, hmm? We'll ask his parents."

"Mama?" Naomi said quietly.

"Hmm?" Miss Miriam turned her fake smile to Naomi, but Becca spoke first.

"What happened?"

Miss Miriam's smile fell a little. "Oh, honey, nothing you need to worry about, okay? Just some stuff with your brother—"

"What did Jake do?"

"I don't really think—"

"Miss Miriam, please."

Miss Miriam sighed. "I think you should let your parents talk to you about it when they're ready, Becca."

Becca's stomach churned. It felt like the balls of waffle she had eaten were rolling around and bouncing off the sides like pool balls. "Did he hurt someone?" she whispered.

"Oh, honey." Miss Miriam held out her arms, and Becca stepped forward. Miss Miriam was one of the few people who Becca could stand to hug her. She squeezed tightly and smelled like incense and clean floors, and Becca held on, just for a second, until she remembered that she was supposed to be fixing the problem, not crying into Miss Miriam's shoulder.

She stepped back. "Can you tell us what he did? Please?"

Miss Miriam bit her lip. "There was an incident with the neighbor's cat," she said. Naomi's hands flew up to cover her mouth, and Eitan looked a little queasy. Becca swallowed and tried to look brave. She wasn't sure if Miss Miriam believed it.

"I really don't know any more details than that, Becca," Miss Miriam went on. "And even if I did, I really think you need to speak to your parents."

Becca nodded. "Okay. Thank you for telling me."

"Of course, sweetheart." Miss Miriam reached out and smoothed down some flyaway hair that had escaped from Becca's braid. "Do you want me to cancel my class? I can stay here with you guys." She smiled again, and that time it seemed a little more real. "We could watch movies."

"No, that's okay, Miss Miriam," Becca said. She ignored whichever of her friends was tugging on the back of her sweater. It wasn't like they needed to remind her that it would be much harder to sneak over to see Jake if Miss Miriam were home. "We were going to go to the park. I think it's a good idea for us to get some fresh air."

"Very true," Miss Miriam agreed. "Fresh air can cure all sorts of ills." She made a silly face. "Even if it is only L.A. fresh air. You guys are sure?"

"We're sure, Mama," Naomi said. "You're going to be late!"

Miss Miriam left after another round of hugs. The three of them sat there in silence for a few long minutes. Then Naomi clapped her hands. "Okay!"

she said. "Jake's feet aren't going to inspect themselves! Let's move, people."

It was easier said than done. There was a police car in front of Becca's house when they got there, so they had to stash their bikes behind the fence of one of the neighbors' houses and go around the back way. They peered over the backyard fence. No one was out there, but Becca could see her parents in the kitchen talking to a police officer. It was hard to tell where anyone else was. The twins were probably still at the Weinsteins' house, but Jake had to be home.

"There!" Naomi said. She pointed to the tiny upstairs window that belonged to the bathroom Becca shared with Jake. There was a doll dangling out of it. Not Ariela's new doll, Becca saw with relief, but definitely a doll. It inched toward the ground, and another doll appeared out the window, then another, and another, until a chain of plastic dolls was hanging almost to the ground, tied together by what looked like hair ties.

"He's raiding the bathroom supplies," Becca said dully.

"How did he even get the dolls in there?" Eitan asked.

"Ariela sometimes plays with them in the bath-tub," Becca told him. "She must have left her box in there yesterday."

"Okay, sure," Naomi said. "Why is he doing that?"

"It's not him," Becca said stubbornly. She was sure. "He would never go this far, and he wouldn't keep messing around. He's afraid of the police."

"Aren't we all," Naomi said. "So, how do we get in?"

Becca thought about it. She had never snuck out before, and she had certainly never snuck in. There had never been a reason for her to break rules like that. Jake snuck out sometimes, she knew. She wondered how he usually did it.

"Um, guys," Eitan said. They turned to look at him, and he pointed. Becca sucked in a quick breath, and Naomi smothered a shriek behind her hands.

"Is he climbing down the hair ties?" Naomi demanded.

"It looks that way," Becca said faintly. She hadn't really expected the answer to how Jake snuck out to be climbing down the house on a rope of hair ties.

"Okay, but why the dolls?" Naomi asked.

"Handholds," Eitan suggested weakly.

Becca shook her head. "That can't be how he usually gets out," she said. "He's way too heavy for that to work."

"We better hope he isn't," Naomi said. It was true. Jake was already fully out the window and sliding himself slowly down the makeshift rope. "Or we'll have much bigger problems than—" There was a sharp snap, and Naomi shrieked again. This time she didn't even try to cover up the noise. Becca was already moving, racing across the yard to where her brother was crumpled on the ground in a pile of plastic dolls and hair ties.

"Jake," she yelled. "Jake! Jakey! Are you okay?"

She almost fainted with relief when a groan came from the pile, and Jake shifted to lie on his back. His foot was bent at an odd angle, and there was a bubble of blood rising from where he had bitten his lip, but Becca couldn't see anything else obviously wrong. She dropped to her knees next to him.

"Jake?" she said again.

His eyelids fluttered. "Becca? What happened?"

"You fell out the window, stupid," Becca told him.

"The window?" His face crinkled up like he was confused. "Why was I going out the window?"

"That's a great question!" Naomi said, coming up behind them. "I'm going to look at your foot, okay, bud? Why don't you tell us what you were doing?"

Jake shook his head slightly. "Nae?"

"Yeah, bud, and Eitan's here too."

Eitan sat down on Jake's other side and patted his shoulder gently.

Jake blinked at him, then turned back to Becca. "I don't know what I was doing. The last thing I remember is getting that stupid gift card for the first night of Hanukkah."

Becca froze. "That was last night, Jake. You don't remember anything after that?"

Jake shook his head, then hissed out a breath when Naomi chose that moment to pull his shoe off. Eitan and Becca both turned to look as she peeled off Jake's sock to reveal a perfectly normal, already swelling foot. Naomi clicked her tongue and stripped Jake's other shoe and sock off as well.

"Normal feet," she announced. "Though that one looks like it's going to be as big as a watermelon in a few minutes."

"Normal feet?" Jake asked. "Why would you—" His words cut off with a strange gurgle, and his eyes rolled back until Becca could only see white between his fluttering eyelids. His foot slid back into place with a click, and the swelling on his lip disappeared, leaving only dried blood behind. Then he started to laugh, only it wasn't Jake's usual snorting laugh. This laugh was lower and made goose bumps race up Becca's arms. Her skin buzzed, and panicked whispers filled her ears as Jake sat up and cracked his neck.

"Normal feet," he said in a voice that was clearly meant to be making fun of Naomi. "You've been reading too many stories, kids." Jake stood up and shook himself like a dog getting something off its fur. "Why would I have to take his place when I could just take *him*?"

12

INTERNET EXORCISMS ONLY WORK ONCE

"A dybbuk," Eitan whispered.

"Like on the bus?" Naomi asked. Jake was still twitching and laughing. Becca wondered if maybe the dybbuk was a little more shaken up from Jake's fall out the window than it had expected.

"Worse," Eitan said. "This one doesn't seem like it's stuck like the other one was. And it's possessing Jake."

"We need to get him somewhere so you can do the exorcism thing again," Becca said.

Naomi's eyes were wide in her face. "How?"

Becca looked at her brother. His eyes were

still rolled back in his head, but he had stopped shaking. He was just standing there, occasionally twitching, so Becca did the only thing she could think of. She slapped him, hard, across the face. Naomi yelped, but Jake's face went slack and his eyes started to move. Becca slapped him again and then one more time. The third time she hit him, Jake slumped a little and shook his head. He scowled up at her. His eyes were back to normal.

"Oh, you are so grounded, Becks. You know you're not allowed to hit me."

"You hit everyone all the time," Becca said automatically. Then she rushed forward, peering into her brother's face. "Are you Jake?"

Jake shoved at her. "Who else would I be? Geez, you are so weird." He looked around. "What am I doing down here?"

"You're supposed to go to the park with us," Naomi said quickly. "The police are here, and your parents don't want you to talk to them."

"The police?" Jake grabbed on to Becca's sleeve. She held very still so she wouldn't automatically shake him off.

"Yeah," Eitan said. "And they're for sure going to want to talk to you, so we need to go right now."

Jake kept hold of Becca as he followed them through the back fence and over to where they left their bikes.

"Get on the handlebars," she instructed him.

Jake did. It said a lot for how nervous he was that he even let Naomi buckle a helmet on him first, but Becca wasn't counting on this sudden bout of following directions to last. Jake, even when he was on his best behavior, wasn't great at doing what he was told. Becca took off before he could change his mind and jump down off the handlebars. She heard Eitan and Naomi call after her, but she trusted them to follow.

Becca took them to the far side of the park, where there was no parking lot and a dense group of overgrown trees. She prodded Jake off the bike and made him sit on a stump. Jake blinked up at her. Becca looked back at him for a moment. Then she knelt and tied his shoelaces together, then pulled the string out of his sweatshirt and used that to tie his wrists together. Finally, she pulled the string out of her own sweatshirt and looped that through the ties at his wrists and ankles, connecting them so he wouldn't even be able to hop on his tied feet. That seemed to snap him back to himself more than anything else had, and he wiggled and complained, but Becca wasn't willing to take any chances. She ignored her brother's whining, though she patted him on the shoulder in sympathy when she finished.

"It's just in case," she told him. He glared up at her from his hunched-over position on the log. Becca bit her lip to keep from laughing at him. "We're going to do something to try to help you, but I think you're going to try to run away."

"I won't run away!" Jake told her.

"Okay, maybe not *you*, but I think the thing inside you that we're trying to get rid of might try to make you run away."

"There's a thing inside me?" Jake asked. He looked shocked, and Becca tried to figure out the best way to explain it.

She was saved by the arrival of her friends. Jake immediately turned to Eitan. "There's a thing inside me?" he repeated.

Eitan nodded, still slightly out of breath. "Yeah. It's called a dybbuk. Sort of like an angry ghost. It's possessing you."

Jake looked impressed. "Cool."

"Not cool," Naomi corrected. "Very dangerous."

"And very mean," added Becca.

Jake shrugged. "All right, not cool. So, what? You're going to call a priest or something?"

Becca rolled her eyes. Naomi opened her mouth like she was about to go off on a lecture, but Eitan cut her off. "It's a Jewish ghost," he said. "We're not looking to get priests involved."

Jake made a face. "All the movies have priests," he said.

"You're not even supposed to be watching those movies," Becca reminded him. "Now be quiet and let Eitan work."

Eitan held up his phone, the screen already showing the words he had used on the dybbuk last time.

"You're going to get it out of me?" Jake's voice sounded small all of a sudden. Like he was just realizing how scared he should actually be.

"We're going to get it out of you," Becca said firmly.

"Okay. I believe you." Jake hooked one of Becca's feet between his tied ones, anchoring her to him. Then he held out his hands to Naomi, who squeezed his fingers between hers. "Ready," Jake said.

Eitan squared his shoulders and began to read.

Becca held her breath as Eitan finished reading with a flourish. Then they all looked at Jake.

He shrugged. "It tickled a little, I think?"

Eitan pressed his lips together. "Well, it took a couple of tries last time." He lifted his phone again and started reading from the beginning, louder this time. Halfway through, Jake started to laugh. He kept laughing, and then the laugh turned into the other one, the not-Jake one. Eitan kept reading, but Becca could already tell it wasn't going to work. The dybbuk didn't even seem upset, and her skin was itching worse than it had at the house.

"Again, Eitan," Naomi said, casting a nervous look at Jake. She still had his hand clutched between hers; her knuckles were white with the force of her grip. Eitan took a quick drink from his water bottle and started again.

He got through it three more times before Jake even started to sweat, and was getting ready to begin again when Becca cut him off.

"It's not working," she said.

Eitan gestured at the still-laughing Jake. "It's doing something." It was true. Jake was sweating harder, and his hand was shaking in Naomi's, but it was nothing like how the dybbuk on the bus had reacted.

"Not enough," Jake said. He looked up with a smile, and even though it was technically her brother's face, Becca felt like she was looking at a stranger. Becca slid sideways away from him, and Naomi dropped his hand and scrambled backward, but the dybbuk was only looking at Eitan. "You don't have the power to use those words properly," the dybbuk said. "I know about the one on the bus. A stranded, weak, hungry thing." He leaned toward them, pulling against the flimsy restraints of shoelaces and sweatshirt strings. "I'm not stranded or weak." The grin widened. "But I am *hungry*."

The dybbuk lunged forward, snapping its teeth. The knots on the shoelaces pulled tight, and Becca was sure they wouldn't hold for long.

"Come over here," Becca said. She pulled Naomi and Eitan a safe distance away, making sure to keep an eye on the dybbuk. "We have to do something else," she said.

Naomi cast a nervous glance at where the thing that wasn't Jake had begun contorting its neck to try to chew on the shoelaces around its wrists. "Did you have something in mind?"

Becca gestured at Eitan. "The dybbuk said you don't have the power to use the words. Who does?"

"A rabbi, right?" Naomi said. "Though I'm not sure that Rabbi Levinson learned how to do an exorcism in rabbinical school."

"Maybe it's an elective," Eitan joked weakly.

Becca shook her head. "We can't tell Rabbi Levinson."

"We don't know any other rabbis, Becks," Eitan reminded her.

"Then we have to figure it out," Becca said. "We don't need help. We *shouldn't* need help. We've fought off demons before, and we're grown-ups now. Everyone keeps saying so."

Naomi made a noise of frustration that made Becca flinch. "What is your obsession with being a grown-up, Becca? And why, why, why do you think we can't ask for help? Grown-ups ask for help!"

"They do," Eitan agreed. "That's kind of part of being mature, you know, Becks? Knowing how to ask people for help."

Becca wasn't sure they were right, but she could see how there might be *some* truth to their words. Still . . . "We can't ask Rabbi Levinson," she repeated. "He'll just call our parents."

"We *do* know another rabbi . . . ," Naomi said.

Becca started to ask "Who?" And then stopped. "You can't be serious."

"What?" Eitan asked.

"And anyway, how will we even get to Santa Clari—" Becca stopped. "Oh. Jonah."

Naomi grinned at her.

"What are you talking about?" Eitan said. "And what about Jonah? I think it's weird that you're friends, by the way. He doesn't even hang out with *me* that much."

"It's because you don't know how to appreciate star maps," Becca said primly. "You just care about planets. And the *moon*. Anyway, Jonah will drive us to Santa Clarita."

"What's in Santa Clarita?" Eitan asked. Then his eyes got huge. "Oh no. No, Nae, absolutely not."

Naomi nodded firmly. "Rabbi Gershon will help us," she said. "And I bet he knows how to do an exorcism, too."

"Can a ghost even perform an exorcism?" Eitan said. "Wouldn't that, like, banish it, too?"

"That's even assuming we can still see the ghosts," Becca reminded them. "And how do we explain to Jonah that we're bringing along my tied-up little brother?"

Naomi shrugged. "He's your friend. Do you think he'll care?"

"He won't even notice," Eitan muttered. "He's worse than Becks when it comes to things he doesn't think are important." Becca pinched him, and he slapped at her hand. "What? I'm right."

"Guys," Naomi warned. "I hear sirens."

"There's no way," Eitan said. The three of them stopped for a moment and listened. There were, actually, sirens getting closer, but it was L.A. That didn't necessarily mean anything. The sirens got louder and then began to fade away as the police cars passed them by. They all let out a breath.

"I'll call Jonah," Becca said.

At this point in their friendship, Jonah didn't require very much explanation or warning from Becca when she needed a ride somewhere. Becca sometimes wondered what he got up to when he wasn't doing his research. He never seemed to be that busy.

"He doesn't do anything," Eitan said. "He literally just does his research and builds star models."

"The star models are cool," Becca said. The star models *were* cool. Jonah built them in his parents' garage. He had started with a scale model of the solar system that took over half the ceiling—he had covered everything in black felt to give him a good backdrop to start with. Everything was correct down to the millimeter. Becca had measured it once. Jonah's newest project was the Milky Way 3D-printed in individual stars and clusters that he was embedding in an enormous disc of clear resin. He was going to rig it with a light underneath so it would project a reverse image of itself onto the felt ceiling. Becca couldn't wait until it was finished.

Jonah pulled up in his van a few minutes later, honking like he always did when he arrived. "Hello, gremlins. The taxi is here," he called out the open window. "Why is he tied up?"

Becca glanced back at Jake and then toward Naomi. "He did it himself, and he won't let us cut them," Naomi said quickly. "He swears he can get the knots." She made a face that Becca recognized as an expression Naomi's mom often wore when she was talking to other parents about something silly the kids had gotten up to. "We're letting him try," Naomi told Jonah.

Jonah shrugged. "Long as he can wear a seat belt."

"Definitely." Becca shoved Jake into the back next to Naomi and clambered in after him. She had warned the dybbuk to be quiet, for all the good that would do, but so far it didn't seem like it wanted to talk to Jonah. That was more than fine with Becca.

"You good, Little B?" Jonah asked. He had started the car but hadn't put it into drive yet, and he had turned around in his seat to look at Becca. "You seem"—he frowned at her, clearly trying to figure out if something was wrong—"like you're not so good."

"I'm good," she told him.

"Al right." He turned back around and put the car in gear. "Santa Clarita, huh? You know, I asked about your aunt Ruth who was out there making pizza. Your mom said she lives in Calabasas."

"She just moved," Naomi said quickly.

"Sure," Jonah said. "So, where am I going this time? Got an uncle you need to see?" Becca bit her lip. Jonah didn't usually ask them so many questions. Though she didn't usually ask him for rides so far away, either. "I'm just messing with you,"

Jonah said before Becca could think of a story. "Hey, I got the Pleiades done today!" He reached his fist into the back seat, and Becca obligingly bumped it with her own.

"The Seven Sisters, right?" she asked.

"Right," Jonah said. He was smiling. "Way more than seven stars in the actual cluster, though."

"This is your exit," Eitan said loudly.

Jonah smiled at Eitan too. "I'll get you there, bud, no worries." He pulled onto the exit, and Eitan turned the radio up.

The drive didn't take long, given how bad the traffic could get sometimes. Jonah pulled into the temple parking lot. Becca was relieved that it wasn't empty—she didn't think any of them could come up with a lie that would convince Jonah to leave them in an empty parking lot outside a closed temple.

"Great. They're here already!" Naomi said brightly. She gestured vaguely at one of the other cars as she hopped out and pulled Jake out behind her. He had stayed sullenly silent the whole ride, but Becca could feel the prickly magic pouring off him, so she knew the dybbuk was still in control.

"Thanks, Jonah," Becca said, scrambling out

after them. Eitan joined them on the curb. "I'll see you next week!"

"No problem, kiddo. Cousin." He fist-bumped Eitan through the rolled-down window. "Be safe!" He honked the horn once and drove away.

They turned to face the temple.

Becca took a deep breath. "Let's go find out if we can still see ghosts."

13

JAKE BARGAINS
WITH DEAD PEOPLE

The temple was quiet when they slipped in the
front doors, but Becca could hear the sound of
someone's shoes clicking against linoleum down
one of the hallways. They hurried Jake across the
lobby and into the sanctuary. Becca was relieved
to find it empty; the dybbuk had started groaning
and muttering as soon as they entered the temple.
It was already beginning to grow dark, and the
pews cast long shadows as the kids settled against
the back wall of the sanctuary to wait for night.
Naomi pulled out the bag of sandwiches she had
packed them for dinner and passed them around.

Becca inspected the two she had been given and decided that it would be easier to feed Jake a cheese sandwich than a peanut butter and jelly, despite the fact that she really would have rather eaten the cheese herself.

"If you can hear me in there, Jake, you better be grateful," she told him. The dybbuk only glared, and Becca forced herself to roll her eyes like she wasn't terrified of being so close to it. Magic was still rolling off it in prickly, horrible waves that made Becca clench her teeth against the force of it. "Stay quiet or I won't feed you."

The dybbuk glared harder, but its wordless protests died away. Becca held out a small piece of sandwich. "If you bite me," she warned, "I'm going to eat the rest of this myself. Jake can survive skipping a meal."

The dybbuk snapped its teeth once, then opened Jake's mouth so Becca could carefully toss a bite of sandwich into it. The dybbuk stared at her balefully as it chewed. "Do you really think this will work?" Its voice sounded odd, like a blend of Jake's usual whininess and something very much not human but full of rage. "I've been feeding on souls for hundreds of years. No rabbi alive now will know the words of power you would need to banish me."

Eitan snorted quietly, and Naomi bit her lip. Becca just smiled a little. "That could be true," she agreed.

"So, why are you wasting my time like this? Your brother is almost gone. He has proven a very hospitable host." The dybbuk bared his teeth and leaned toward Becca. "You didn't like him anyway. Let me have him, and I'll leave you out of it. It'll just be between you and me."

Becca frowned at the dybbuk, confused. "What does liking him have to do with anything? He's my brother. I'm *responsible* for him."

"What do you mean, between you and her?" Naomi cut in. "Who would you tell?"

The dybbuk shrugged. Becca held up another piece of sandwich and it opened its mouth.

"Why did you choose Jake?" Eitan asked.

The dybbuk shrugged again, but Becca was beginning to catch on as well. "You didn't, did you?" she said slowly. "That would be too much of a coincidence."

Again the dybbuk stayed quiet, but it smiled slowly, unchewed sandwich oozing between its teeth. If it had really been her brother, Becca would have scolded him for being gross. As it was, the effect was almost frightening. "He called to me," the dybbuk said. "He was so open to being influenced."

"I believe you about that," Becca said. "Jake is the worst. I just don't think you would have known to come looking for him in the first place without someone pointing you our way."

The dybbuk mimed zipping its mouth shut, then laughed and immediately opened it again in a silent demand for more sandwich. Becca fed him a piece absently, meeting Naomi and Eitan's worried looks.

Later, Naomi mouthed, and Becca nodded. It probably wasn't smart to talk about these things in front of the dybbuk. They were planning to banish it, but she had no idea what happened to dybbuks after they were exorcised. Maybe it would just go right back to whoever had sent it. She was sure, though, that it *had* been sent. Just like the tiny mazzik and probably the toilet demon as well. But by *who?*

Eitan tapped his fingers against her elbow, and she turned to look at him. He offered her a smile she was pretty sure was meant to be reassuring.

"Later," he whispered. "We'll figure it out."

The dybbuk cooed at them and made kissy noises. Becca shoved the rest of the sandwich into its mouth. She figured it was invested enough in keeping Jake's body alive that it wouldn't let him choke.

"Well," a calm, deep voice said above them. "I didn't expect to see you all again." There was a low chuckle, and Becca turned to look into the wise, slightly transparent eyes of Rabbi Gershon. The ghostly rabbi looked exactly the same as the last time Becca had seen him. He was still dressed in his temple clothes, with his tallit wrapped around his shoulders and a smile tucked into his prominent beard. It was strange to be so comforted by the appearance of a ghost, but Becca was mostly just relieved that they hadn't imagined him during their crazy adventure with the Golem. Rabbi Gershon swept his eyes over their group. "What have you children brought me this time?"

"Rabbi Gershon!" Naomi stood up quickly and moved toward the ghostly rabbi like she was thinking of hugging him, then realized that wasn't going to work. She beamed up at him instead. "We weren't sure we'd be able to see you this time!"

The rabbi stroked his beard. "Well, here I am. And who is this?"

"That's Jake," Becca told him. "He's my little brother. He, um, he has a dybbuk."

Rabbi Gershon made a surprised noise and leaned forward to peer at Jake, who pulled a ridiculous face at him. Jake—the dybbuk—looked like it might be getting worried, though. Its eyes were wide enough that Becca was almost afraid they would pop out of Jake's head. Clearly it hadn't expected a ghost.

"A dybbuk." Rabbi Gershon hmmed and stroked his beard. "A difficult case. I assume you tried to banish it yourself?" he asked Eitan.

Eitan nodded. "Lots of times. It didn't work."

Rabbi Gershon hmmed again. "Well, we have all night. Let me find my books." He flickered out of sight for a second, then reappeared a moment later on the other side of the sanctuary, where the extra siddurim were kept. He began to pull books off the shelves in a movement that left Becca confused for a moment—the shelves weren't any emptier, even after Rabbi Gershon had removed several from different places—until she realized that the books Rabbi Gershon was stacking in his arms were translucent as well, and many different sizes, nothing like the uniform row of identical prayer books.

"Ghost bookshelves," Eitan whispered behind her. "Cool."

"What kind of books are those?" Naomi asked loudly.

The rabbi gave them a small smile. "Oh, research and prayers and whatnot." He spread the books on the podium that stood in the center of the bimah. "Let's see, now. Tell me what you've been noticing with your brother."

The dybbuk chose that moment to start crying loudly. "Please, Rabbi Gershon," it called out in Jake's voice, wobbly and tearful. "Please, there's nothing wrong with me! I don't know why they tied me up and took me here, but I haven't done anything wrong! Get them to let me go!"

Rabbi Gershon raised his eyebrows at them. Eitan cleared his throat awkwardly, and Naomi grimaced. Becca just raised her eyebrows back.

"Not typical behavior from your brother, then, Miss Reznik?" the rabbi asked. He was ignoring the dybbuk's continued wailing in the background, so Becca did her best to ignore it too.

"No," Becca said. "Jake doesn't cry *or* say please."

Amusement twinkled deep in the rabbi's eyes, but his expression stayed grave. "I assume the dybbuk didn't make him more polite in general."

Becca shuddered. "No, it didn't." She swallowed once, looking to her friends to see if one of them might be able to explain, but Naomi just flapped her hands encouragingly at Becca. "Jake's always bad," she said. "Well, maybe not bad, but he's in trouble a lot, and he plays a lot of tricks on people." She thought about it. "He bites a lot," she added.

"I see," Rabbi Gershon said. "So, how did you know something was wrong?"

"He got really, actually *bad*," Becca told him. "He started trying to scare the munchkins—I mean, our little siblings—for real, and he broke their toys on purpose, and he tried to break the menorahs. He knocked the menorah table over and almost caught the kitchen on fire." She wrapped her arms around herself and gripped her elbows with the opposite hands. "He hurt the neighbor's cat."

The amusement was gone from Rabbi Gershon's face, leaving only gentle concern. He patted Becca's shoulder. It felt cool and soft, like a bag of frozen peas. "He became cruel," the rabbi said quietly. Becca nodded miserably, and the rabbi patted her shoulder again. "We'll fix it," he said.

Rabbi Gershon moved back over to the podium and opened several of his books, laying them out all in a row so he could look between them. Becca, Eitan, and Naomi crowded around him, but Becca realized as soon as she got close that they weren't going to be able to read them. It wasn't just that the books were written in Hebrew, which they definitely were, it was that the pages were all translucent. The letters shifted and blended with the pages below them and seemed to fade in and out of existence depending on whether Rabbi Gershon was looking at them or not. The rabbi seemed to read them just fine, though, and made lots of thoughtful noises as he turned pages and went from book to book, stroking his beard as he read. In the corner, the dybbuk seemed to have realized that the begging and pleading wasn't going to work and switched to making as many loud, gross noises as it could. Jake would have found the farting sounds hilarious. Becca put her hands over her ears and tried to tune it out.

The rabbi read for long enough that Becca and

Naomi had settled into the chairs along the back of the bimah to doze, and the dybbuk had started to flag in its attempt to be as annoying as possible, only blowing the occasional raspberry at them whenever they accidentally caught its eye. Otherwise, it was back to gnawing at the shoelaces that bound Jake's wrists and ankles together. Only Eitan still stood next to the rabbi, squinting and craning his neck like he could read the pages of the ghostly books if he just looked at them the right way. Finally, Rabbi Gershon lifted a large book from the podium and turned to face Becca.

"I believe I may have found the solution," he said, "but it will not be pleasant for your brother."

The dybbuk started laughing again, and Becca swallowed around a sudden tightness in her throat. "Do it," she said.

Rabbi Gershon nodded. "We need a minyan. If you would," he said to the air.

Naomi yelped and grabbed Becca's wrist as people began to appear around them. There were ten in all, dressed in white like they were going to temple on Yom Kippur and draped in sparkling tallitot. They crowded around Rabbi Gershon on the bimah and peered at the books, commenting to one another in whispery voices.

"My friends," Rabbi Gershon said, "we have a young man here who needs our help." He nodded toward Jake, who bared his teeth at the crowd and hissed. "There is a dybbuk possessing him, and the words alone are not enough. Will you help?"

Everyone started talking at once. Becca caught a few cries of "that poor boy," and one or two comments about how it had been a long time since anyone had seen an exorcism. The consensus seemed to be that yes, they would help.

Becca let out a breath. "Thank you," she told the group. That set off another round of well-meaning chattering and reassurance before Rabbi Gershon cleared his throat.

"Are we ready?"

The group didn't get any quieter, but they did move to form a half circle around where Jake and his dybbuk were leaned against the wall. The rabbi handed out ghost books to everyone and pointed out where they would need to begin reading. Then he went back to the bimah. "You can come closer, if you'd like," he told Becca and her friends, "but you must not interrupt. Do you understand?"

"What are you going to do?" Becca asked.

The rabbi sighed. "There are several things we could attempt, if we need to. Many of them I would rather not subject your brother to. First we're going to try to strike a bargain."

"A bargain," Eitan repeated. "You're going to try to get it to make a deal with you? Isn't it just trying to cause as much damage as possible?"

Rabbi Gershon stroked his beard and smiled. "Dybbukim are certainly agents of chaos," he agreed, "but most often they are also souls with unfinished business."

"Like . . . they died right in the middle of doing something?" Naomi asked.

Rabbi Gershon twinkled at her. "More like they have sins to atone for or have committed an act for which they need to repent. We will offer to help them do that."

"How?" asked Becca.

The rabbi *hmm*ed and shrugged a little. "Maybe he wants us to say Kaddish for him or give tzedakah." He gestured toward the velvet-covered donation box at the door of the sanctuary. "Sometimes these things are enough."

"And if it's not enough?"

"Let us confront that question when it becomes

relevant, Becca, and remain hopeful until then. What do you say?"

Becca nodded slowly. Naomi shifted closer and tightened her grip around Becca's wrist, and Eitan pressed his shoulder to hers on her other side. They moved like that toward the pews just outside the half circle of ghosts and sat together. Becca rubbed her hands up her arms. She wasn't sure if it was the dybbuk's presence making her itchy or the worry she felt for Jake. Either way, it felt terrible.

They watched Rabbi Gershon step into the center of the group so that he was standing over Jake. Jake blinked dully up at him, then started to smile. The grin stretched until it was wide enough to show nearly all of Jake's teeth—it looked painful, and Becca wasn't sure Jake would have been able to smile like that if there weren't an evil spirit controlling his muscles. Rabbi Gershon ignored him, and the dybbuk started pulling more grotesque faces, trying to get his attention, until Becca was afraid Jake's face was going to crack from the tension. When that didn't work, the dybbuk started writhing, pulling against the tied shoelaces and shrieking bad words and horrible accusations.

It seemed to know the community members by name and was talking about horrible things they all might have done when they were alive. Becca was impressed at how calm they all still were. The dybbuk wasn't even talking to her, and she was shaking. Or maybe that was Naomi. They were pressed close enough together that it was hard to tell, but Becca was so overwhelmed with everything that the closeness didn't even bother her.

"Begin," Rabbi Gershon said. The group started chanting a prayer that sounded a lot like the one Eitan had tried to use to banish the dybbuk, but it was longer and had a complicated, wailing tune that reminded her of a shofar being blown. Rabbi Gershon spoke to the dybbuk in Hebrew, his low, rumbling voice weaving in and out of the chant like it was a part of it. The dybbuk screamed and convulsed, yelling things in Hebrew that Becca didn't understand and some things in English that she wished she didn't.

The third time through the prayer, the dybbuk sat up and locked eyes with Becca. Fat tears rolled down its face. "Becks," it pleaded—and she had to think of it as an *it*, or she wouldn't be able to leave it sitting there—"Becks, please, stop them."

"You're not Jake," she whispered. "You're not my brother. You're trying to steal him from me."

"Bebe, it hurts!" it cried.

Becca clenched her fists tight enough that her nails dug into her palms. Jake hadn't called her "Bebe" since he was six, but it had been the only thing he had called her for years. Just hearing the nickname in his voice made her automatically want to reach out to him. "You're not my brother!" she repeated, trying to put more force behind the words.

The dybbuk stopped crying, though it kept staring at Becca, twitching occasionally when the ghosts' chanting became more forceful. "Stop them, and I'll tell you who sent me," it called. "He's been watching you. Don't you want to know why?"

Becca looked to Eitan. He sucked his bottom lip into his mouth, thinking hard, but then he shook his head. "No," he said. "We'll figure it out. Jake is the important thing right now."

"And who knows if it'll even tell the truth," Naomi pointed out.

"I will! I'll tell you everything!" The dybbuk screamed something in Hebrew at Rabbi Gershon. "Stop them!" he yelled.

"Give me back my brother!" Becca shouted.

Rabbi Gershon's voice grew louder, and the dybbuk was forced to turn back to him. They went back and forth in Hebrew for a while, until the dybbuk was flushed and sweating and Rabbi Gershon seemed like maybe his ghostly form was beginning to fade a bit. Finally, after Becca was sure the exorcism wasn't going to work after all, Rabbi Gershon gave the group of ghosts some sort of signal, and the prayer changed. Becca recognized it immediately.

"Mourner's Kaddish?" Eitan whispered. "That's really what the dybbuk wanted?"

Naomi shushed him. Becca couldn't turn to pay attention to either of them. She was too busy watching Jake's body slowly droop until he was lying on the floor in a position that might have looked relaxed if not for the shoelaces shackling his wrists and ankles. There was a crackling noise and a feeling like thunder in the air. Jake convulsed once, hard enough that his head *thunked* against the carpet. Then there was a loud bang, and he slumped backward. His right shoe had a hole in the toe that was smoking slightly.

Rabbi Gershon turned toward them. Becca was

surprised that a ghost could look so exhausted. "It's done," the rabbi said. "The dybbuk has been properly mourned by a community and has found rest."

"That's it?" Becca asked.

The rabbi chuckled. "I don't know if I would be quite so dismissive," he said, "but yes, it's over."

Eitan started asking questions, but Becca didn't wait to hear any more. She ran over to Jake. He was still unconscious, but his eyelids were beginning to flutter. Becca pulled her pocketknife out and sliced through the ties at his wrists and ankles. Naomi was close behind her. She pulled the smoking shoe off his foot.

"Look," she gasped. Becca leaned over to see what Naomi was pointing at. The big toe on Jake's right foot was a bloody mess. It looked like the time one of Becca's teammates had crushed her toe with their cleats. The nail had come clean off, and the skin around it was bruised and oozing.

"It's where the dybbuk exited his body," Rabbi Gershon said, coming up behind them. "It looks painful, but it's a good sign. It means the spirit is really gone."

Becca nodded, then looked at Naomi, who

nodded as well and started pulling Band-Aids out of her backpack, looking for one big enough to cover Jake's toe. Becca turned back to her brother.

"Jake? Jakey, can you hear me?" She patted at his face until his eyes blinked slowly open. He stared hazily up at her.

"Becca?"

"Yeah, bud."

"Did you get the thing out of me?"

Becca smiled at him. "Yeah, Jake, we got it."

Jake lifted a hand and punched her lightly in the arm. "Cool." His head dropped back, and his eyes shut again.

"Let him rest," Rabbi Gershon said. He was frowning now. "We should discuss what the dybbuk told you. If it was telling the truth, I worry your troubles will only continue to grow."

14

JAKE TAKES
THE BLAME

They talked with Rabbi Gershon until the sun started to rise, Jake dozing fitfully against Becca's shoulder. Rabbi Gershon was worried, and he only seemed to get more worried as they told him about the things that had been happening at Becca's house.

"It's not unheard of," he said thoughtfully, "for certain mischievous beings to be drawn to people experiencing turmoil." He gave Becca a kind, sad smile. "And it does sound to me like things have been tumultuous for you lately, my dear."

Becca felt her eyes burn. She nodded, and Rabbi Gershon patted her hand.

"The thing that worries me," the rabbi went on, serious again, "is that usually it's singular spirits, like your dybbuk, or chaotic demons, like your mazzik. It's rarely so . . ." He pressed his lips together.

"Organized," Eitan filled in for him.

"Quite so," Rabbi Gershon said. "That, along with the Golem and its . . . counterparts, paints a worrying picture. It leads me to believe that there is something larger at work here, though it is hard to say what."

The three of them looked at one another. Naomi was gnawing on her lip, and Eitan was shuffling his feet like he couldn't keep still. Becca knew how he felt. The rabbi's worry made her stomach churn. She tapped her hands against her legs, but the small movement wasn't enough to settle the anxiety. She swayed a little, the movement taking her in and out of Naomi's space. Naomi gave her a tight smile before turning back to Rabbi Gershon.

"How do we find out more?" Naomi asked.

Becca added, "And how do we stop it?" since that seemed like the most important question.

Rabbi Gershon stroked his beard. "How you stop it will depend on what it is," he said. "And finding out what it is"—he spread his hands in front of him—"that's a difficult thing to manage. There are only a few entities in our mythology that would have the power or inclination to do something like this. I will recommend some books," he said decisively.

"Thank you," Becca said, "and thank you for Jake." She turned to look at her snoring brother. "He's terrible, but I really didn't want to let the dybbuk have him."

Rabbi Gershon smiled again. "Any time I can be of assistance, Rebecca, you need only ask."

Naomi nudged her. The smug *I told you so* in her actions as clear as if she had said it out loud. Becca's eyes were hot again, and she blinked rapidly. She had to swallow several times before she was able to whisper, "Thank you."

Rabbi Gershon faded as the sun finished rising. The four kids trudged to the front doors of the temple, Becca and Naomi supporting Jake between them, and Eitan clutching the list of recommended reading materials.

They sat on the curb in front of the temple, leaning against one another and squinting against the sun.

"We'll figure it out, Becks," Eitan said. "I won't do anything else until I've found the solution for you, I promise."

Becca leaned over and lightly tapped the sides of their heads together. It was all the affection she could muster just then, but it made Eitan laugh, so she figured it was okay.

"Whose parents do we call?" Eitan asked.

Becca let out a long breath. "Mine," she said. "We have Jake."

Naomi frowned. "I think maybe we should call mine. They'll drop us off at your house and we'll tell your parents Jake ran away to stay with us."

"It won't work," Eitan said. "Your parents will know Jake wasn't there, and your mom won't like us lying when Jake's in trouble and there are police involved."

"We can't get grounded now, though!" Naomi protested. "We have work to do."

They sat in silence for a long moment, thinking. Then Becca said, "I have an idea. Jake," she said loudly. Jake grumbled quietly but otherwise didn't stir, his head still heavy on her shoulder. "Jake," she said again. "Wake up!" She shook him, and he flopped off her shoulder and jolted up, startled.

He blinked muzzily at her. "Huh?"

"We're going to blame you," Becca told him.

Jake blinked again, scrunching up his face. "For what?"

"For us being all the way out here. We're going to say you took off and hopped a bus, or something, because you were afraid of the cops, and then you called me because you were lost, and we called Jonah to take us out here to pick you up."

Eitan whistled. "That's a pretty good lie, Becks. I'm impressed."

"It's not *that* much of a lie," Becca muttered.

Naomi tapped her chin. "Why didn't Jonah just wait for us?"

"We weren't sure where Jake was, and Jonah had to get to the lab," Eitan said immediately.

"Why me?" Jake demanded, fully awake now that there was talk of him being in trouble.

"We're only out here because of you in the first place," Becca reminded him. "It's not *our* fault you were so horrible a dybbuk got you and no one noticed." Jake flinched at the mention of the dybbuk, and Becca felt a little bad, but she didn't take it back.

"We'll cover for you with the cat," Naomi offered. "We'll say you saw some other kids with it and took it from them but didn't know what to do, and then when the cops came, you were too scared to say."

Jake's frown lightened a little with that.

"Will they believe it?" Becca asked doubtfully.

Naomi scoffed. "Would you believe *I* was lying to protect someone who hurt an animal?" she shot back.

That was fair. Of all of them, Naomi was always the most willing to get people in trouble if she thought they were hurting other things on purpose. If it had actually been *Jake* who hurt that cat, Naomi wouldn't have even checked on him when he fell out the window.

"It could work," Eitan said. "We'll still get in trouble for not calling, though."

"Less trouble than we'd be in for harboring a fugitive and running away," Naomi pointed out.

Nobody could argue with that, so Becca made the call, though she handed the phone to Naomi as soon as it started to ring. Naomi grinned at them when Becca's mom picked up, already yelling frantically. Then she made her eyes big and wide and sad, like Becca's mom could actually see her through the phone. "It's Naomi, Mrs. Reznik," she said, her voice small and wobbly. "We found Jake. We're in Santa Clarita. Could you"—she sniffed loudly—"could you come pick us up?"

Becca's mom fussed and scolded and hugged them all. She shook Jake a little and demanded to know why he hadn't just told them what happened in the first place, then rolled her eyes with exasperation when Jake just shrugged. Becca thought they would have been in more trouble if they hadn't all looked so exhausted and scared. As it was, she just got her own little shake from her mom.

"Next time you need to call us *before* you go chasing after your brother!" her mom said. Then she crushed Becca against her in a very tight hug. Becca tried not to squirm. Usually her mom was more careful about Becca's limits for physical contact, but Becca knew it had been a hard day for everyone. "You did good," her mom said quietly. "Thank you for looking after him."

Becca nodded against her mom's shoulder, and her mom let her go, trying to pretend she wasn't wiping at her eyes. "Okay," she said, "everyone in the car. You all had us worried sick. I thought you'd learned your lesson after the last time you disappeared for your geocaching adventure." She rolled her eyes a little, and Eitan looked down at his feet, flushing red.

"We're sorry," Naomi said.

"Sorry," chorused Eitan and Becca.

"I know. And you meant well," Becca's mom said. She shooed them all into the car and went around to get into the driver's seat.

All in all, it could have been much worse. Becca and Eitan were dropped off at Naomi's house, since everyone seemed to think they had disappeared for noble reasons and Becca's parents wanted some time alone with Jake anyway. Naomi's moms were waiting for them out front. Miss Miriam started fussing over them immediately, demanding to know if they'd eaten or if anyone was hurt or needed to meditate with her. Miss Rebecca just stood there with her arms crossed. Becca saw her lift one eyebrow when Naomi met her eyes, but otherwise she didn't say anything and let Miss Miriam herd them into the kitchen and start making them breakfast.

"You all need to bathe," Miss Rebecca said, "and then I think you need to stay in the house the rest of the day."

"Mom!" Naomi started.

Miss Rebecca held up a hand. "You're lucky you're not grounded for the rest of the break, Naomi Sarah. If Mrs. Reznik hadn't called and told us what was going on, you would be. The least you can do is stay where we can see you for the next twenty-four hours." Naomi looked ready to argue anyway, but Miss Rebecca shook her head. "If you try to fight me on this, it'll be two days in the house, and Becca will go stay at Eitan's without you."

That wasn't exactly a threat she could follow through on with the Snyders' new sleepover rules, but Miss Rebecca had a way of making things happen that didn't seem possible. Naomi shut her mouth and accepted a glass of orange juice from Miss Miriam with a scowl. Becca shifted. There was a strange tension building in the kitchen that was different from the tension that came with the magic, but it made her skin tingle in a similar way.

"Great!" Miss Miriam said, throwing a sparkling smile at her wife. Miss Rebecca smiled back, just a little. "It'll be fun, guys! We'll have a movie marathon or something!"

Becca started to agree, but Naomi cut her off. "Eitan has research to do," she said. "We said we'd help him, so we can't watch movies."

Eitan looked as disappointed as Becca felt at the idea of giving up a movie marathon with Miss Miriam to read about demons, but Naomi was right. They needed to solve this as quickly as possible.

"Sorry, Miss Miriam," Eitan mumbled. "I'm doing a project for Rabbi Levinson. He wants me to present it for the fourth graders."

Becca held her breath as both of Naomi's moms looked them over closely, then looked at each other for a long moment. Becca's parents did that sometimes, had conversations without talking. Becca could never figure out how that worked. Finally, Naomi's moms stopped looking at each other, and Miss Miriam smiled again, though it was smaller this time.

"Well, that's really nice of you, Eitan," she said. "And you're definitely a good choice for teaching the younger kids." She reached out and patted Eitan's hand. "You're so smart." She turned back to the stove, humming a little. Miss Rebecca gathered her things to go to work—she worked most weekends—but stopped to give them all one last long stare, like she was telling them that if they tried to escape upstairs before they had eaten enough for Miss Miriam to stop worrying about them, they really would be in trouble. Miss Rebecca was good at giving looks that communicated very clearly. Becca used to think it was a lawyer thing, but Eitan's dad couldn't really do it.

They all nodded at her, and Miss Rebecca nodded back, then went over to say goodbye to Miss Miriam. Naomi whined loudly at them for kissing in front of her food. Miss Miriam laughed and kissed Miss Rebecca again, just to make Naomi yell, "Gross, Mama!" and whatever tension Becca had been feeling disappeared. She let out a long breath that she hadn't realized she was holding and accepted a plate of scrambled eggs and turkey bacon from Miss Miriam. They weren't in trouble, and Eitan had his list from Rabbi Gershon. They were going to figure it out.

15

EITAN FIGURES IT OUT

Becca and Naomi tried to help with research. Eitan gave them both lists of topics to search and set them to work. Mostly, the internet turned up scary stories and horror movies that Becca knew weren't going to be helpful. She was willing to bet that most of the people making them hadn't ever even read about the history of Golems or dybbuks, let alone met one in real life.

By one in the morning, only Eitan was still going strong. Naomi had curled up at the foot of her bed with her tablet under her head and was snoring softly. Becca's eyes were starting to blur even after she moved herself and her fluffy blanket to the floor to try to stay awake, and she found herself having to read whole paragraphs over as she nodded off. After the fourth time she started a page again, Becca decided to close her eyes for a moment, so that she wouldn't miss anything.

She woke up to the smell of toast and a crick in her neck from sleeping slumped over on the floor.

"Oh good, you're up!"

Becca blinked a few times and pushed herself up onto her elbows. There was bright sunlight streaming through the window, and her tongue felt thick and fuzzy in her mouth. She made a face and reached for her water bottle, swishing some water around in her mouth. It didn't help as much as she hoped, but it was better than nothing. Finally, she sat up all the way and looked at Eitan. He was eating a thick slice of challah covered with butter and jam, which explained the toast smell, and looked like he hadn't slept at all. There were dark circles under his eyes, and even though his hair was buzzed short, it had a sort of static quality to it that made Becca sure Eitan had been rubbing his hands over it.

"Listen, I think I've found something. Or maybe

two things. I'm not sure. Two things that could be it, but obviously it's not two things happening. Or maybe it is? Maybe everything is actually unrelated? Oh gosh, that would make things a lot harder. No, I'm pretty sure it's one of these two things."

Becca stared at her friend. "None of that made any sense," she said.

"What?" Eitan blinked at her. "Should we wake up Naomi? I think I've found something."

"You said that already," Becca told him. "I think you should nap. You didn't sleep at all last night, did you?"

"Couldn't," Eitan mumbled around another bite of challah. "But it's okay. Miss Miriam let me have coffee."

"She did not," Naomi said sleepily.

"Nae!" Eitan cried. "You're with us!"

Naomi rolled to squint at him. "Mama didn't give you coffee. She says kids can't have caffeine because it stunts our growth."

Eitan shrugged and took a sip. Naomi sat up. It looked like she was gearing up to yell.

"You said you found something?" Becca interrupted before her friends could get even more dramatic.

Eitan immediately snapped his attention back to his computer. "Yes! Two possible somethings!" he said.

"Stop," Naomi said. "If we're going to have to figure out what's going on between two possible options, my brain needs carbs. I'm getting toast."

Naomi flounced out the door, and Becca could hear the squeak of the handrail that meant Naomi was going down the stairs. Becca went to brush her teeth.

When she made it to the kitchen, Naomi was sitting at the counter with her mama, swinging her feet and looking smug. "Mama gave Eitan decaf," Naomi said.

Becca shrugged at her and sat down at the counter as well. "Good morning, Miss Miriam," she said.

"Good morning, sweetie," Miss Miriam said. She winked at Becca over her own cup of coffee. "Don't tell Eitan. He looked like he needed encouragement."

Becca nodded, and Naomi rolled her eyes but agreed. "Excellent," Miss Miriam said. The toaster dinged, and she got up and handed Becca and Naomi each a plate with two perfectly browned slices of challah. "Butter, jelly, and peanut butter in the fridge," she said. "I've got to run some errands, but Deena is home if you need anything." She kissed the top of Naomi's head, then the top of Becca's, then pointed at them both. "Don't leave the house."

Naomi sighed loudly. "Yes, Mama. Come on, Becca, let's go to my room. Where we'll stay. *All day.*"

Becca grabbed her plate and followed Naomi, grimacing apologetically at Miss Miriam as she walked by. Miss Miriam just smiled at her and made shooing motions.

Upstairs, Eitan was nodding off over his computer. There was a half-eaten bite of toast in his slightly open mouth.

Becca poked his head. "Chew."

Eitan startled so badly the bite tumbled onto his computer. He grabbed it and shoved it back into his mouth, chewing quickly and swallowing while Naomi and Becca made noises of disgusted horror.

"I'm awake," Eitan said.

"You're gross," Naomi shot back.

Eitan rolled his eyes and took a big swallow

of his coffee. "I also have answers, I think." He waited until Naomi and Becca had settled on the floor with their own food and turned his computer around. "Okay, there are two possibilities at play here. There's one I think is more likely, but . . ." He chewed on his thumb for a moment before shaking himself. "Let me just show you." He pulled up a web page that looked like it hadn't been updated in ten years. Becca recognized it as one of the approved encyclopedia sites their history teacher let them use for school projects.

"All right, things started with the Golem, so that's where *I* started." He pointed at a paragraph that Becca didn't have a hope of reading from where she was sitting. "Basically, it's all stuff we already knew. Only great rabbis or sages can create Golems, and they have different functions in folktales, but everyone agrees that things can, well, get out of hand." The three of them shared a long moment of silence as they all recalled just how *out of hand* Naomi's Golem had gotten.

"Anyway," Eitan said, "according to the Talmud, sages and rabbis who study Kabbalah can sometimes perceive spirits and demons around people. And we know that rabbis can do exorcisms, so it wouldn't be crazy to assume that really great rabbis could control certain demons, at least a little."

"So there's a . . . rabbi . . . making my house haunted?" Becca asked.

Naomi frowned. "Why?"

"There's not really a reason that would be happening," Eitan agreed. "The only rabbi we really know is Rabbi Levinson, and he wouldn't do that." Eitan paused for a second. "Also, I don't think he actually could. He's definitely a good rabbi, but I'm not sure he counts as a *great* one. There aren't any great sages around anymore."

Becca huffed. "If you didn't think that was true, why did you tell us?"

"I'm just trying to share all the information!" Eitan protested. "And I don't think you're going to like the second option."

"I already don't like this," Becca said.

Eitan sighed. "Fair enough. The other possibility is that there's a demon interested in you."

"There are lots of demons interested in Becca," Naomi said. "We've seen three of them just in the last week."

"Right," Eitan said, "but all of them had been *sent*. We think. Hard to know with the toilet demon, but it would be an awfully big coincidence if there was just a random toilet demon at the same time other demons were being sent to Becca's house."

"Eitan," Naomi said.

"Right," Eitan repeated. "Sorry. So there's really only one demon I can find in the stories that has any control over all the other demons." He clicked over to a page that was covered in sketches and storybook font. "Ashmedai."

There was a long pause.

"Who?" Naomi asked.

"*Ashmedai,*" Eitan repeated. "The demon that replaced King Solomon? We talked about this when we were dealing with Jake? Come on, guys, Cantor Debbie definitely read us this story at day camp."

"We stopped going to day camp when we were, like, eight," Becca reminded him.

"So you don't remember anything that happened five years ago?"

"Just tell us, Eitan," Naomi cut in.

Eitan took another long gulp from his coffee cup—Becca rolled her eyes at the way Naomi snorted at him—and pointed at his computer again. "Ashmedai is the king of the demons. He was captured by King Solomon to help build the Temple, since King Solomon wasn't allowed to use anything made of iron, which sort of limited his options, you know? So he heard about this worm"—Eitan turned the computer toward him and squinted at it for a moment—"the shamir, which could cut through anything, but he didn't know where to find it, so he had to ask the demons."

This was starting to sound familiar to Becca, but she wasn't sure what it had to do with her house being haunted.

"Anyway," Eitan went on, "a whole bunch of stuff happens, but Solomon ends up sending a servant to bring Ashmedai to his palace so they can ask him about the worm, and Ashmedai helps him get it, and Solomon builds the Temple with the help of the worm and, some people say, other demons. But eventually Ashmedai tricks Solomon into undoing his chains *and* giving Ashmedai his ring. Then Ashmedai banishes Solomon and takes his place until Solomon is able to make his way home, and his guards realize something is wrong with the Solomon they have living in the palace. So Ashmedai runs away, but Solomon is so afraid of him and his cleverness that he has a bunch of guards around his bed all the time from then on."

Eitan stopped and looked at Becca and Naomi expectantly, like they were supposed to understand the point of his story.

"So?" Naomi asked, and Becca was flooded with relief that she wasn't the only one lost.

"*So*, in the story, Ashmedai torments random people on his way to the palace with Solomon's servant and has fun messing with people's fates. He's also definitely strong enough to command other demons to haunt a house if he wanted to."

"Okay," Naomi said slowly, "so I'm still wondering why that's something the king of the demons would do."

Eitan shrugged. "Seems more likely than a random rabbi deciding he really hates us."

"What about the Golem?" Becca asked. "Could a demon make a Golem?"

"No," Eitan admitted. "But I think if a demon is smart enough and powerful enough to trick King Solomon, then he could probably somehow convince a great rabbi to make a Golem, you know?"

"You just said there aren't any great rabbis anymore," Naomi pointed out.

"Well, no," Eitan agreed, "but Ashmedai could probably have met one at some point and convinced him to make him Golems."

"*Why?*" Naomi asked.

"I don't know!" Eitan cried. "I'm working with what I have!"

"All right," Becca said, "that's fine. It's a theory that fits the facts, sort of. So why would he switch from the Golem to haunting my house? And why wait so long?"

"Because the Golem didn't work," Naomi said. "It was a test, and we passed . . . or failed? He kept sending more to see if we'd try again, but we didn't, so he had to try something else."

"And your house was already full of bad vibes," Eitan reminded Becca. "It was probably easier for demons to get in there."

"Great," Becca said. "So we have the why me and why the demons, but we still don't have the why he's doing this at all."

"Sometimes demons just mess with people?" Eitan said. He made a face like he knew that was a weak explanation, but Becca could admit it was the only thing they had.

"We could ask him," Naomi said. She had taken

Eitan's computer and was scrolling through the story. "We have to face him anyway, and the story makes it sound like he has fun explaining his mischief. I bet he'd tell us."

"Back up," Becca said. "Who's facing him?"

Naomi looked up. Her eyebrows were crinkled in the middle. "We are," she said. She looked at Eitan. "Aren't we?"

Becca stared. "This is a demon that defeated King Solomon! What are *we* going to be able to do?"

"Well, we can't just let your house stay haunted," Naomi pointed out. Becca thought she sounded way too calm about this whole thing, especially when Becca was feeling panic creeping in and making her thoughts go fuzzy.

"That doesn't mean we go fight Ashmedai! I'm sure we could figure out an exorcism for the house or something."

"He might not stop," Eitan said slowly. "He's been poking at us for a year now. Nae might be right."

Naomi shook her hair back. "Of course I'm right," she said.

Becca turned to Eitan. "Okay. How do we stop him?"

Eitan looked at Naomi before responding, which made Becca angry. "Eitan! How?"

"Well, in the stories, Ashmedai is captured first because they outsmart him, and then they're able to see through his tricks because they know Solomon," Eitan said.

That was horrible. Becca felt horrible. She was afraid. She gripped at her elbows, pushing her forearms up under her rib cage to try to get rid of the floaty feelings starting to trickle through her body. "So we're supposed to *outsmart* an ancient demon that managed to trick *King Solomon*? And if we can't, then he's just going to stay in my house?" The pressure on her rib cage wasn't helping. She let go of her elbows to wrap her arms fully around herself and squeeze. Naomi stood up quickly and ran to her closet, pulling down her weighted blanket. She wrapped it around Becca and sat in front of her.

"Breathe, Becks. You won't have to do this alone."

"I don't want to do it at all," Becca whispered. She could feel tears starting to run down her cheeks, and she pushed her face down into the soft fabric of the blanket.

"Okay," Naomi said. "That's okay. You don't have to."

Becca snapped her head up. "Really?"

"Really," Naomi said. She shared a look with Eitan that Becca couldn't understand. Eitan's mouth twisted, and his shoulders slumped, but he didn't say anything. "Really," Naomi said again, more firmly. Then, "I'll do it."

16

IT'S NOT ACTUALLY HANUKKAH GOBLINS

Whatever they were going to do would have to wait. As soon as the weekend was over, Becca's mom picked her up from Naomi's and brought her home. The twins had been retrieved from the Weinsteins' house, so the entire family was waiting. Apparently, it had been decided that what they all really needed was *quality time*. Becca wasn't sure why they thought forced time in the house with everyone would be better for Jake than sending him to a doctor, but she supposed it was hard to explain what had happened. At the very least, the guilty attention was better than the tension-filled quiet. If Becca hadn't had the looming threat of Ashmedai and the constant bombardment of bad vibes from the house to worry about, she wouldn't have minded a few days of board games and movies and cooking together without her mom running out of the room to take calls or her dad locking himself in the office. As things stood, it was making her a little crazy.

"They have tickets to Zoo Lights on Thursday." She was hiding in the bathroom to make the video call. It had been the only way she could sneak away from family Lego building for a few minutes.

"Won't they want you to go with them?" Eitan asked. "They don't seem like they're trying to leave any of you alone right now."

"I'm going to have to lie about it." Becca sighed.

"Will that . . . work?" Naomi asked.

"It should," Becca said. "I'm going to start acting like I don't feel good now, and by the day after tomorrow, it won't be suspicious that I don't feel well enough to go to the zoo." It wouldn't be hard. With the energy in the house, Becca felt dizzy and off-balance most of the time anyway.

"I feel like that makes them less likely to leave you alone," Eitan said.

"It would, but Zoo Lights tickets are expensive," Becca reminded him. "They'll feel bad, but it won't be worth wasting the money right now. This was a big treat for us for the last night of Hanukkah."

"You sure you don't want to go, Becks?" Naomi asked, biting her lip. "We could try to figure out another time."

Becca shook her head. "This is more important. I'll tell them you guys are going to come keep me company so they don't worry."

Naomi was still biting her lip. "Are you sure?" she asked again. "It's the last night of Hanukkah." Then her eyes got wide, and she gasped. "It's the last night of Hanukkah!" she cried.

"Yes?" Eitan said.

"Just like the book! We're facing the king of the goblins on the last night of Hanukkah. I *told* you."

"He's the king of demons, not goblins, and none of the others were goblins either," Becca reminded her.

Naomi wasn't listening. "I wonder if we just have to get him to light the Hanukkah candles."

Eitan snorted. "Well, it's as good a plan as any

of the others we have at this point," he said. "We're not even sure how to summon him."

"He'll come when we call," Naomi said confidently. "He's probably coming anyway, for the eighth night."

"You're insane," Becca told her friend. Someone knocked at the door, and Becca heard her mom calling her name. "I have to go. I'll see you guys Thursday." She hung up and flushed the toilet, then ran the sink for a few seconds. She opened the door to her mother's concerned face.

"You okay in there, honey?"

"Yep," Becca said. Then she was struck with sudden inspiration. She had been worried about acting sick, but . . . "It's just a stomachache," she said. "Probably from all the snacks." Her mom looked worried, but Becca shrugged her off. "It's nothing, Mom."

Over the course of the rest of the day and the day after, Becca made lots of trips to the bathroom, spending longer and longer in there each time and holding her stomach as she came out. By the time Thursday morning came, Becca's parents were more than ready to believe that she had some kind of stomach bug. Becca could see that they were struggling with the idea of leaving her alone, but she was also right about the Zoo Lights tickets. They wouldn't want to waste them.

"Nae and Eitan are going to come keep me company," she said for the third time as her mother hovered and her father guiltily checked his watch. "Eitan even made me biscuits so I can have something soft to eat."

"Okay." Her mom sighed. "But call us if you need anything, or if you start to feel worse. We won't make it a long trip."

"Take as long as you want," Becca said. "I'm really okay. I just don't think I could walk around all night, you know?"

Her parents fussed a little longer, but they eventually took the rest of the kids and went to the zoo, just like Becca knew they would. She swung herself out of bed as soon as she heard the garage door shut and texted her friends.

Coast is clear.

Then she got dressed. Whether it was the king of the goblins or the demons that they were set up to summon, Becca didn't want to face him in her antique map pajamas, even if they were her favorite set. Once she was wrapped in her softest jeans and favorite hoodie, Becca made her way down to the garage and started moving all the toys and boxes out of the center of the space. They'd decided that the garage was the best place to call to Ashmedai, because it had the least number of things that could break. It also meant that they would have almost zero warning when her parents got home, so there wasn't a lot of room for mistakes.

Naomi and Eitan got there just as Becca was finishing clearing a space in the garage large enough that all three of them could stand with room for one much larger person—or demon—to stand with them. Eitan really had brought biscuits, and Becca munched on one quietly while her friends looked around.

"I feel like we should draw a pentagram on the floor or something," Naomi joked, though her voice sounded thin and nervous.

"I don't really know what we need," Eitan admitted. "There's so much different speculation and so little to go on with Ashmedai. They say he lives on a mountain and ascends to heaven to study Torah, but that doesn't sound very demonic to me."

"Demons can't be scholars? Are we not all subject to God?"

Becca nearly jumped out of her skin at the new voice behind them. Naomi shrieked, and Eitan dropped his backpack with a loud clatter. A tall, brown-skinned man with a full black beard was standing in the garage with them, inspecting the twins' Barbie Jeep. He was wearing a bright orange sweatsuit that clashed incredibly with the ancient-looking crown on his head. He turned, making a strange rustling noise, and Becca saw the outline of two very large wings settling behind him before vanishing completely. Her eyes traveled down toward his feet, where one goat hoof and one chicken foot stuck out of either eye-wateringly orange pant leg. Becca didn't need the icy prickling crawling up her spine to tell her this was the demon they'd been planning to summon.

Ashmedai followed her gaze and smiled. "I can never get the feet right." He squatted down to peer into the tiny rearview mirror of the Jeep. "The face though, that's a work of art, if I say so myself." He looked up at them. "Don't you think?"

"Um. Yes. Sir," Eitan said. "It looks wonderful, sir. Who is it?"

"What's with the 'sir'?" Naomi muttered.

"He's a king," Eitan hissed back. "You have to be respectful."

Ashmedai smiled and inclined his head toward Eitan. "From one scholar to another," he said, "I thank you. And this face is someone I thought you'd be familiar with. A comforting figure from your history. Do you not recognize him?"

"You just look like a guy," Becca said. Eitan shot her a frantic look over his shoulder, but she ignored it. Ashmedai had been tormenting them for more than a year; she wasn't interested in being polite to him.

Ashmedai's smile turned sharper. "This face is Solomon's," he said.

Eitan squeaked, and even Becca felt a jolt of surprise. Naomi was staring with her mouth open. "Can we take a picture?" Eitan asked. "I mean, it's just that no one actually knows what King Solomon looked like. There's not even a description in the stories."

"Why do you want a picture?" Becca asked. "It's not like anyone will believe you. And who says he's not lying, anyway?"

"Becca!" Eitan cried.

"She's right, though," Naomi said.

"I'm not lying," Ashmedai said mildly. "This is Solomon. Though of course he didn't dress this way." He turned side to side like he was admiring his horrible sweatsuit in a mirror. "The clothes these days are so much more fun."

Naomi faced the demon, angling herself so she was in front of Becca and Eitan. "What do you want from us"—she glanced sideways at Eitan's pale face and added—"sir?"

Ashmedai stopped plucking at his clothes and turned to inspect Jake's old softball gear. "How is your brother, Rebecca? He's an interesting child, isn't he?"

Becca lunged forward, but Eitan caught the back of her sweatshirt, and Naomi shook her head hard. *Let me deal with it,* she mouthed.

"You're not evil," Naomi said to Ashmedai, "not really."

"Thank you."

"But you are *tricky,* and even if none of the stories quite line up, you always want something."

Ashmedai tilted his head like he was thinking about nodding but wasn't quite sure he wanted to. "Knowledge, mostly," he said. "Power. To see overconfident, self-righteous *kings* taken down a notch or two." His form flickered a little, and Becca saw the outline of a much larger, much more monstrous shape for a moment before Ashmedai's Solomon face settled back into place. "The world is so small these days, and my shedim are so *ineffective.*" He trailed his fingers along the edge of the workbench with all the family's power tools on it. "Men are the same vain, selfish creatures they always have been, but they have the means to do so much more evil with their petty whims." He turned back to them, making a face like he was telling them a secret. "If there were ever a time for a flood."

"You sent the Golem to flood L.A.," Naomi accused.

"I sent the Golem to *you*," Ashmedai corrected. "*You* sent the Golem to flood L.A."

"How did you get the Golems?" Eitan asked

Ashmedai waved a hand. "I've had them for millennia. You weren't the only one I sent one to, Naomi. You weren't even the only one who tried to wake one up. But you *were* the only one who actually managed it. I was *very* interested in that. It takes a fierce kind of faith and righteousness to wake up a Golem. Then you destroyed it. What a shame. It did what I needed it to do, though, so no harm done." He smiled at them again.

"What did you need it to do?" Naomi asked.

"Faith is an interesting thing," Ashmedai said, like he hadn't heard her. "Faith, belief, is its own kind of power. Most people can't see demons, you know."

"We *know*," Becca said. "The Golem's magic did that."

"Did it?"

"Stop confusing us," Becca demanded.

The smile grew. "That's what I *do*."

"Will you leave us alone?" Naomi asked.

"No," Ashmedai said simply.

"Why?"

"Did you know," Ashmedai said, "that there are very few places in the world where people still have a healthy fear of me and my shedim? All sorts of unrighteous, *wasteful* men, and no worry about the demons who would gather at their funerals and remind God of their sins."

"Okay," Naomi said. "So?"

"It's sundown," Ashmedai observed, looking out the small windows in the garage doors.

"Oh!" Naomi said, her voice suddenly much

higher. "Should we light candles? It's the eighth night!"

Becca and Eitan looked at each other. Naomi had insisted that they try to get Ashmedai to light Hanukkah candles like in the book, just in case. Becca had had her doubts, but it was the only plan they had just then.

"We have them set up right here, actually." Naomi gestured over-dramatically toward the folding table where they had set up Becca's menorah.

"Such thoughtful children." Ashmedai went over to the small table and picked up the matches. He struck one and lit the shamash candle. Then he took the shamash delicately between his fingers and lit all the rest of the candles. "Will you say the prayers?"

Eitan cleared his throat and stepped up. He recited the prayers from memory, keeping his eyes on Ashmedai the whole time. When he finished, a huge wind began to blow around them. The garage darkened and Ashmedai roared, his shape shifting into that horrible shadow again, but this time it stayed that way. He thrashed and screamed in the wind, and Eitan, Becca, and Naomi clung to one another and waited. Finally the wind died down, and the light returned. The garage was empty and quiet again, the darkness outside still tinged with pink and gray from the fading sunset.

"Just like the book," Naomi whispered. She whooped. "I knew it would work!"

Becca was shocked that it had worked. She rubbed at her arms, waiting for her skin to stop prickling a warning. It didn't usually take this long, but maybe Ashmedai's magic lingered longer than the other demons'. He was definitely different from them, and Becca thought he must be more powerful.

"Wow," Eitan said. "He actually was a Hanukkah goblin." He grinned around the garage, looking very impressed. "Way to go, Nae." He held out his hand for a fist bump, which Naomi gave him, smiling back.

"I knew it," Naomi said again.

"There's that faith."

The three of them screamed as a huge, writhing shape faded into view in front of them. Ashmedai had gotten rid of Solomon's face and was now in what Becca thought must be his true form. He was huge and looked like several different animals melded together, with the wings of a bat on his back that looked large enough to reach past the top of Becca's house if he unfurled them.

A smile stretched across his ugly, bulbous face. "Gotcha."

17

BECCA FACES
HER DEMONS

Two days before they faced Ashmedai, Eitan had
gotten them all on video chat and told them everything he could find about demons. Just like everything else in Judaism, there were a lot of rules
about demons. Most of them were about the things
that would draw demons to people, but Eitan had
read dozens of stories that had other rules too.
There were rules about which demons caused specific problems, what to do if a person ended up
brought into a demon's home, where demons were
allowed to live, and, in one interesting story, the
legal rights demons had in the community. Becca

loved rules. Rules made sense. They stayed consistent and helped her know what was expected of her. Becca could work with rules. She just wasn't always sure how to make the rules work for *her*.

In the garage, under the fluorescent lights that cast everything in a dull orange, Naomi was pale and shaking, but she kept her position in front of Eitan and Becca, her eyes locked on Ashmedai. Becca tried to think, but she wasn't good at this kind of thing. She could hear Eitan's voice in her head saying *it's about the ability to sense subtlety and nuance* and could see the face Naomi made when she knew Becca wasn't understanding something and didn't know how to explain it.

Demons used twisty thinking to confuse people into sin. All the heroes in the folktales used twisty thinking to outsmart the demons. That was always the way. Becca had grown up with those stories and had never seen herself in them. She wasn't Hershel of Ostropol, outsmarting eight nights' worth of goblins to save Hanukkah. She wasn't even one of the fools in Chelm, so silly that she accidentally looped back around into cleverness. She was Rebecca Reznik, mapping the universe in Jonah's garage because every single star had its place. She didn't fit in this story. She couldn't follow these rules.

"Tell us what you want," Naomi shouted.

"I already have," Ashmedai said. His voice had changed with his body. It was higher, and there was a hissing underneath it when he spoke that made Becca shudder.

"Tell us how to stop you," Eitan tried.

Ashmedai laughed. "Would you believe that I've told you that, too?"

Eitan sighed, and his familiar exasperation was almost a comforting sound. He didn't sound afraid at least, though the way his hands were shaking made Becca think he was maybe just pretending. "Unfortunately, I would believe that," Eitan said.

It made Ashmedai laugh again. It wasn't a very nice laugh. Naomi started to ask another question, but Becca had stopped listening. She needed to *think*. If Ashmedai had already told them why he was there and how to stop him, then it just meant they had missed it. That was fine. Becca was practically a professional at going back over conversations in her head to see what she had missed. It was one of the reasons she was so good at remembering what people said. She had to, so she could correct herself if she got something wrong the first time. She just had to find what Ashmedai had told them.

Eitan yelled something. It sounded like he was trying the exorcism he had tried on the dybbuk. Becca wasn't sure why he thought that would work. Maybe he was stalling for time. She was shivering, she realized. She kept going over everything Ashmedai had said, but the way her teeth were chattering was distracting. It felt like spiders were crawling all over her. It was getting worse. The wave of magic she could feel growing wasn't like anything she had felt so far. Even the dybbuk had felt like nothing compared to this.

"The world is so small these days, and my shedim are so ineffective," Becca whispered to herself. "If there were ever a time for a flood. It takes a fierce kind of faith and righteousness to wake up a Golem." A crackle of fear ran down her spine. She looked up at Naomi, her eyes bright and her face flushed, trying to bargain with the king of the demons for their lives, because she had promised Becca she would. *"There's that faith.* It was a test," she muttered. Then, louder, "It was a test!"

Everyone turned to look at her. Ashmedai was smiling.

"What was a test, Becca?" Naomi asked.

"Everything," Becca said. Her breath was coming fast now; she felt like she had been doing sprints at softball practice. It was hard to force the words out when all her senses were screaming at her that she needed to get somewhere dark and quiet and safe. She dug her nails into her palms. "The Golem came first. Ashmedai wanted to know if anyone could do it. It wouldn't work if they couldn't wake up the Golem."

"*What* wouldn't work?" Eitan demanded. Becca flinched back a little from the volume of his voice, and his face twitched, but he did get quieter when he repeated, "What wouldn't work?"

"Any of it," Becca said. "The demons showed up after the Golem because Naomi passed the first test. Ashmedai has been sending them the whole time." She looked at the demon king, who had shrunk down a bit and was now holding a shape somewhere between Solomon's face and Ashmedai's monster form. It was kind of awful to look at, but there were so many thoughts spinning in Becca's head, she didn't have room to be afraid of anything else. "Right?" she asked him.

Ashmedai's smile didn't change, but he shrugged

a little. It was honestly more of an answer than Becca had expected.

"The world is so small these days, and my shedim are so ineffective," Becca repeated. "It takes a fierce kind of faith and righteousness to wake up a Golem. It wasn't the bad vibes that brought the demons to my house," she said. "Lots of people's houses have bad vibes. Way worse than mine. It was that we *expected* them."

"No, we didn't," Naomi said. She had moved closer, still keeping herself between Becca and Ashmedai, though Eitan had managed to inch forward to stand shoulder to shoulder with her. Normally that would bother Becca, but she didn't think Ashmedai was actually going to hurt them.

"Yes, we did," Becca reminded her. "Remember? As soon as I told you home was making me itchy, you were sure there were demons, and then the first demon showed up that night. *You* have the faith, and *we*"—she gestured between herself and Eitan—"have faith in *you*." She turned and pointed at Ashmedai. "And *he* needed a door. They all needed a door. Can't you feel them?" The magic—the demons—were now so close that Becca felt like she was more goose bump than girl. She would have ripped her sweatshirt and jeans off and stood there in her socks and underpants if she thought it would have helped at all, but she knew from horrible experience that there wasn't really anything she could do to get rid of the sensation except get rid of the magic. And she was working on that part.

Naomi's eyes were wide, and Eitan's face looked frozen. They were surprised, Becca realized. They hadn't noticed how much worse the horrible magic feeling had been getting. Neither of them had spent the last few minutes trying to focus while fighting the urge to crawl out of their own skin. That was almost the most shocking thing about the whole situation, and Becca had the strangest urge to laugh. Her friends were so *weird*.

"Okay," she said, "well, now you've noticed. He's bringing them, but he can't do it by himself. He's not really that powerful."

"Excuse me," Ashmedai said, though he didn't sound mad. Becca knew what mad sounded like. Weirdly, he sounded kind of proud, which couldn't be right, but Naomi was looking at him a little oddly too, so maybe it was.

Not evil, Becca remembered. *Just twisty.*

"Well, you're not," Becca said. "You're not like . . . the devil. You're just a very smart, very old, very powerful"—she thought back to the stories—"but not totally immortal . . . guy?"

Ashmedai's smile was smaller now, but it felt less scary like that. "And?" he asked.

"And you want to help," Becca realized suddenly.

"He what?" Eitan shouted. Becca flinched again, but Eitan didn't seem to notice that time.

"He wants to help," Becca repeated. Doubt was beginning to prickle at the back of her head as her friends just kept staring at her. She wasn't used to doing the explaining for things other than *her* things. But she was sure about this one. Mostly. "Don't you? 'All sorts of unrighteous, *wasteful* men, and no worry about the demons who would gather at their funerals and remind God of their sins,'" she recited. "You want people to be righteous again, but you needed help to bring the shedim back out of the . . .'" She trailed off, trying to remember what one of the stories—the one that had made Naomi laugh because the demons had gone to court—had said about where demons lived. "The 'dark forests and wastelands.'"

"You want to punish people like you used to," Naomi said, and Becca felt a rush of relief that her friend had finally caught on. If Naomi was getting it, then Becca was almost definitely right.

"I'm a *scholar*," Ashmedai said, pressing one of his scaly hands to a place that might have been a chest on a slightly more human body.

"But you're also a king," Eitan said, "and not all the demons are scholars. They have other purposes."

Purposes. Rules. Becca chased the thoughts around her head, trying to put them in an order she could make sense of. Judaism loved rules, so Jewish demons loved rules. They followed the rules each time they defeated a demon, but they had tried the candles with Ashmedai, and that hadn't worked. Maybe that hadn't been his rule. As far as Becca could tell, though, Ashmedai himself didn't have many rules, just tricks. Becca grabbed fistfuls of her hair, messing up her braid with how hard she was gripping, but she needed to *think*, and it was that or scream. She wanted to be in a different garage, with a map of the Milky Way and precise scale measurements for everything. She wanted to be where things made *sense*.

"You can't *make* the world behave," Naomi was saying. "We learned that the hard way with the Golem. Didn't you pay *attention*? There's too much wrong now, and the world is too complicated."

For some reason that reminded Becca of something Jonah had said to her, the last time she was over at his place helping with his Milky Way project. She had been upset about her family and talking about how things should just stay how they were supposed to be, like the stars do. Jonah had laughed a little, but not *at* her. He never laughed *at* her. He understood. He'd explained how that wasn't really how stars worked—it was hard for burning balls of gas to stay exactly the same all the time—and then he'd said, *Every star has its place, Little B, but the universe is constantly expanding.*

Becca looked up and met Ashmedai's eyes. She usually only did that with people if she absolutely had to, but this felt even more important than that. The demon king's eyes were very human looking, and if Becca didn't look away from them, she could almost pretend he was just another grown-up. "The universe is constantly expanding," she told him. Ashmedai tilted his head at her. "You can't make things smaller again just because it would be easier. You can't make everything stay the same even if change sucks. That's kind of a rule."

Then she had it. "There's another rule, in all the stories about demons," she said. She looked at Ashmedai. "You know it too, don't you?" Ashmedai mimed zipping his lips. Becca whirled around and pointed at Naomi. "You believe in the stories, right? You have *faith* in them?"

Naomi nodded. Becca held out her hand, and Naomi looked a little surprised but didn't hesitate to take it. Becca held her other hand out to Eitan. "And you're sure that the stories are right? You got us good information?"

Eitan scoffed. "My information is always good."

It was such an *Eitan* reaction that Becca felt less overwhelmed for a moment. She laughed, more just a burst of air than a sound, but it helped. "Okay, Eitan, sorry." She turned back to Ashmedai. "You know the rule of the stories," she said again. The rule was this: At the end of the story, humans won. Every time. Even if it took generations for righteousness to come back and push out the demons. Humans always won.

Becca didn't have faith like Naomi, and she wasn't clever and witty like Eitan. She wasn't good at being subtle or at understanding nuance, and she didn't like things that felt bad, no matter how much they may be good for her in the long run. But she knew how things were *supposed* to be. She could follow rules. She believed in rules. And with her friends on either side of her, it was easy to believe in this one. "We win," she said simply.

Ashmedai flinched. Becca felt Naomi's hand tighten around hers.

"We've always won, over and over again, forever. You can lead us wrong, and you can trick us, and you can get us twisted around, but you can't stop us from finding our way back."

Maybe she was imagining it, but the hammering pressure of the magic seemed like it was getting easier to bear. Becca kept talking. "We've won so much and so often that you don't belong here anymore."

Ashmedai had shifted back to Solomon's form, with his mismatched demon feet and the orange tracksuit that was honestly just as demonic. He held his hands out to Becca. "Listen, Rebecca, let's discuss—"

"No, *you* listen," she said quickly. She couldn't risk letting him confuse her again. She bit her lip and thought of the way Naomi had cried for her Golem and the way Eitan was always taking in new information, trying to meet Becca's needs and Naomi's high expectations of him. She thought of her dad's tired face and her mom's anger and the way Jake had looked so scared when he realized the horrible things the dybbuk had made him do. "We're a little twisted around right now, like, as a species," she admitted, "but we're going to find our way back, and we're going to win, and *you don't belong in our world anymore*." She put all of her certainty behind those words, just like she had been certain that the incantation would get rid of the toilet demon, that the mazzik should be visible, and that that *darn tree* wasn't supposed to be on the path. The same way she was certain that the coming year was going to be a hard one, but her friends would make it easier. The way she was certain that she wasn't totally ready to be a grown-up, but she was getting there.

Ashmedai was tugging at his beard and looking between the three of them like he was trying to decide who would listen to him. The magic had faded to pins and needles instead of scraping claws. Becca took one more deep breath. "People don't need your kind of help anymore. You don't belong in our story." She stepped forward, bringing Eitan and Naomi with her. "It's time for you to go."

There was no wind this time. No roaring or darkness. It wasn't that kind of story anymore. Ashmedai was there one moment, looking at her with a complicated expression, somewhere between a smile and a scowl, that Becca wasn't even going to try to understand. The next moment he was gone, and the magic was gone with him. Completely.

Becca dropped her friends' hands and let out a long breath of relief when she realized that for the first time in weeks, her skin wasn't prickling at all. Naomi let out a shout and leaped at Eitan, dragging him over so the two of them in their victory hug could lean against Becca's back. Becca swayed against them, laughing in surprise when Eitan hooked a hand into her hoodie and spun her around so she could jump up and down with them. She stopped them when they got too close to the table with the Hanukkah candles on it. Becca caught her breath, looking at the familiar menorah with its colorful candles. They were melted down to stubs, but still burning. Outside the garage windows, the stars were coming out.

18

A REBOOT

The telescope was the best Hanukkah present Becca had ever gotten, even if it was technically Eitan's Hanukkah present. The natural, quiet darkness of the forest they were camping in was a huge relief after all they'd been through over the past couple of weeks. Things had been weird. There weren't any more demons in Becca's house, and no pins and needles warning Becca of something magical getting too close. There was no magic at all. In fact, the more they investigated, the more it seemed like there had never *been* any magic at all.

Naomi's Golem graveyard was empty, just a clean patch of flat earth that looked like it had never been disturbed. Jake didn't remember the dybbuk or their trip to the temple to see Rabbi Gershon. Becca asked her mom and dad about the broken dam last year, and neither of them had known what she was talking about. They hadn't remembered any of the weird occurrences that had led up to it either, or the situation with the bathroom door, which was good as new. The neighbor's cat was fine too. Even Rabbi Levinson had stopped watching them so closely at temple, which was good, even if Becca kind of missed the attention.

Only Becca, Eitan, and Naomi seemed to remember anything strange happening in the last year.

"It's like you fully rebooted the universe," Eitan had said, sweaty and dirt streaked from digging in Naomi's garden plot for much longer than it actually took to know that it was empty. "A clean slate. No magic. No demons."

Becca couldn't tell what the tone of his voice meant, but he hadn't seemed mad. Naomi wasn't mad either. They were all just . . . tired. The camping trip helped. It felt normal. They loaded up all their gear into the Snyders' camper van—and

Becca absolutely did not think about the time the Golem set up their tent in the backyard in under three minutes—and packed their bug spray and all their snacks. Eitan brought his well-loved *Backyard Astronomer's Guide* with its forest of Post-it notes sticking out the sides, and Becca brought her new copy of National Geographic's *Space Atlas*—a Hanukkah gift from Jonah—and Naomi brought her pocket guide to edible wild plants, and they didn't worry about being hunted by demons in the woods.

Mr. and Mrs. Snyder stayed in the camper, and Becca, Naomi, and Eitan piled all their stuff into the tent and raced off into the woods to track down as many edible plants as they could until it was dark enough to stargaze. They had dinner that Mr. Snyder cooked over the fire pit—Naomi smugly added a wild greens salad that Becca took three bites of out of loyalty to her friend—and then spent the hours until the eclipse picking out constellations and eating the marshmallows they'd brought for s'mores straight from the bag.

It was later than Becca had ever stayed up before. The total eclipse didn't even start until two in the morning, but this was special. They pushed and shoved good-naturedly over who got to use the telescope to look at the moon first. It was Eitan, of course, but Becca didn't mind. She was used to sharing, and the eclipse lasted long enough that everyone would get a turn. And besides, she could see the moon just fine without it. Naomi pressed her shoulder against Becca's in the dark, leaning against her to keep balanced while she tipped her head back to look at the sky. Beside them, Eitan was staring through the telescope, describing everything he could see in detail and sharing facts about eclipses. Becca took a bite of a marshmallow and watched the moon turn red above them and thought that maybe not *all* the magic was gone from the universe after all.

They went to bed full of sugar and giddy with excitement over the eclipse. Becca listened to the buzz of the crickets and other nighttime bugs outside and the quiet, not-quite-asleep breathing of her friends huddled together under a pile of sleeping bags in the tent that they were beginning to outgrow.

"I think I get it," she whispered.

"Get what?" Naomi whispered back.

"*Spiritual maturity*, or whatever," Becca said.

She rolled over onto her stomach, pulling the sleeping bags over their heads so she could turn on their camping lantern without Eitan's parents spotting the light. Eitan made a garbled noise of complaint from Naomi's other side, but slid down so his head was under the sleeping bag too. Becca stuck her tongue out at him, and he scowled back.

"I'm tired, and it's *so* late," Eitan complained. "Can we have our spiritual revelations in the morning?"

"Technically it *is* morning," Naomi pointed out.

Eitan turned his scowl on her. Naomi pointedly faced away from him and looked toward Becca. "What do you get, Becks?"

"I don't have to think about things a certain way." Becca rolled the words around in her head for a bit, thinking about what she was trying to say. "Like, I'm never going to be *subtle* or *nuanced*, not the way you guys are, but that doesn't mean I'm never going to be a grown-up."

She looked up at her friends. Eitan's scowl was gone, and he was nodding at her even though he was still blinking sleepily in the lantern light.

"It's about figuring out what grown-up me looks like."

Naomi reached over and hooked her fingers in Becca's sleeve.

Becca smiled at her. "Things are still pretty scary, huh? Even without demons? Not just high school, but everything."

Naomi let out a long breath. "Yeah," she said, "but people are already working on it. *We're* going to work on it."

Eitan pushed himself up on his elbows and grinned at her. "Plus, we've already saved the world twice. How hard could it be to do it again?"

Becca snorted. "Don't jinx it."

He laughed and flopped over onto his back. They were quiet for long enough that Naomi switched off the camping lantern and pulled the sleeping bags back down, reaching over to make sure Eitan and Becca were both fully covered and tucked in. Then she settled back. Becca found Naomi's hand in the dark and hooked their pinkies together.

"We don't have to be grown-ups completely yet, right?" she whispered. "Even if we've had our Bat Mitzvahs and are spiritually mature and stuff?"

"Not even a little," Naomi said confidently.

"Yeah," Eitan said. "Think of how upset our parents would be. They're always talking about how we're getting so big and need to slow down. My mom cried the other day because I got my high school class list from the guidance counselor."

"We'll take it slow," Naomi said. "We've got time."

"And each other," Eitan added. Becca huffed, and Naomi poked him and told him to stop being so cheesy, but he didn't take it back.

Becca smiled in the dark. "Okay," she said. "I think that could be okay."

SAMARA SHANKER has been making up stories about magic and monsters since she was a kid sneaking in extra reading past her bedtime. By graduate school, she had moved on to writing stories that reimagined the folklore and mythology she had always loved as a kid (mostly still written after bedtime, once she finished all her sensible homework). She works now as a tutor and children's literacy specialist, and gets to do most of her writing during the day, which has done wonders for her sleep schedule. She lives in Virginia with her rescue puppy, Jack Kirby, and devotes most of her time not spent working or writing to spoiling her niece and nephew.